THE
BOOK
OF
NIGHT

POEMS OF THE MACABRE

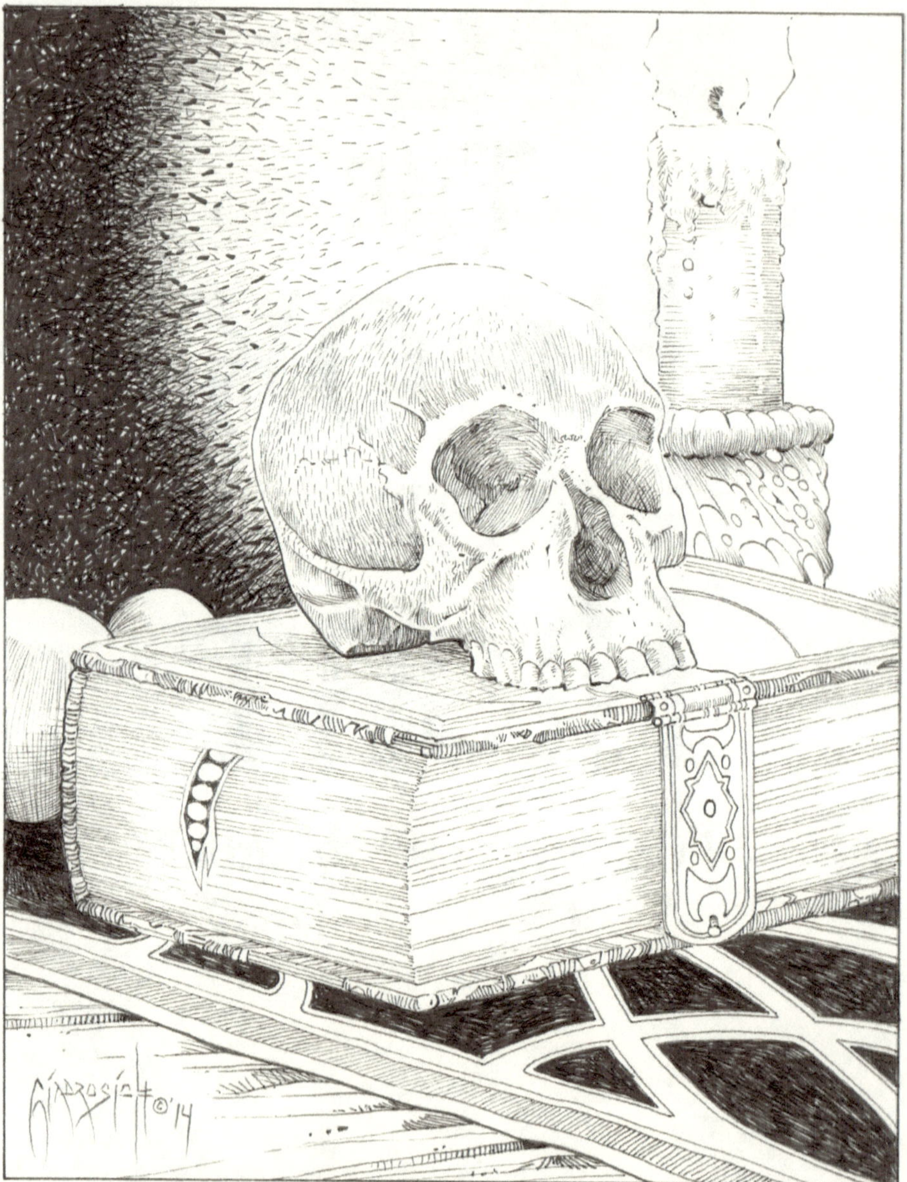

 *THE BOOK OF NIGHT FRONTISPIECE* BY BOB GIADROSICH

The
Book
of
Night

Poems of the Macabre

Edited by Richard Groller

An Imprint of Copper Dog Publishing, LLC

THE BOOK OF NIGHT

The poem *Beloved Warrior* first appeared in the book *The Fish the Fighters and the Song-girl,* by Janet Morris and Chris Morris, © 2010 by Janet Morris, published by Perseid Publishing, 2012.

Published by Moondream Press, an imprint of
Copper Dog Publishing, LLC
537 Leader Circle
Louisville, CO 80027

Visit our Web site: www.copperdogpublishing.com

Credits:
Cover art: *The Garden of Good and Good,*
Copyright © Chris Mars/Chris Mars Publishing, Inc.
www.chrismarspublishing.com

Cover and Interior Design: Helen Harrison

Edited by Richard Groller

Library of Congress Control Number: 2015917125

ISBN: 978-1-943690-01-5 (Paperback Edition)

ISBN: 78-1-943690-02-2 (Kindle Edition)

First Edition: October 2015

Published in the United States of America

CONTENTS

THE CHAPTERS
APPARITIONS

AUTUMN PEOPLE

SWEET SORROW

Through a Glass Darkly

ILLUSTRATIONS

PREFACE

THE BOOK OF NIGHT HAS BEEN OVER 20 years aborning. Originally envisioned as a collaboration between a single artist and a single poet, it evolved into what you see today. Poetry is a labor of love, but a labor generally not well compensated, if at all. When *The Warrior's Edge* was published back in 1990, my co-author Janet Morris graciously shared her literary agent, Perry Knowlton, the president of Curtis Brown Ltd. of New York, with me. Perry perused the nascent *The Book of Night* and to summarize his comments: "It's original, beautiful, but it's poetry–we won't make any money." The same thing happened when the project was brought to White Wolf Publishing, back when I was working staff at World Horror I. Comments essentially the same.

Fast forward 20 years. Janet Morris now had her own publishing company (Perseid Publishing) and offered the opportunity to finally let *The Book of Night* see the light of day (pun intended). We had been working on a lot of collaborative writing projects over the last few years (primarily the *Heroes in Hell* series), so it just felt right to expand the scope of the effort, and include both new voices and departed masters to the mix, in a way that was both enlightening and unique. I hope you will agree.

Unfortunately, very late into the development, we ran into technical difficulties with schedules and formatting and the project once again languished on the backburner.

Luckily, one of the contributing writers we met through the "Hellions", a diehard poet and creator of the *Sha'Daa: Tales of the Apocalypse* series by the name of Michael H. Hanson, decided to found his own publishing company, Copper Dog Publishing, LLC. He offered to take on the project, and Janet graciously agreed for the project to leave the Perseid stable with her blessings. So here we are.

As a collaborative effort, there are many to thank for this project coming to fruition. First and foremost, Michael H. Hanson for believing that the time was right for this to be a viable venture. To Janet Morris for believing in it still after so many years, and resurrecting the vision of what it could be. To Bob Giadrosich, the first artist to put vision to the concepts of *The Book of Night* so long ago, whose unique style is visible throughout the work. My wife, Cynthia (Tish) Groller, who has endured the long wait with me patiently, and has been an astute editor with a good ear. To Helen Harrison for formatting and making the graphics work. To Sarah Hulcy for early technical guidance. To the living poets in our writers group, who had the bravery to expose their souls to the night, I offer my sincere thanks for your participation in this labor of love: Louis Agresta, Larry Atchley, Jr., Jeff Barnes, Dean Drinkel, Richard Evans, Jack William Finley, Allan Gilbreath, Michael H. Hanson, Lori Martin, Janet & Chris Morris, Kurt Newton, Jillian A. Perkins, Kimberly Richardson, Bill Snider, and Angel Weaver. To the artists who gave vision to the poets thought-forms, my sincere thanks to Paul and Michael Bielaczyc of Aradani Studios, Chris Mars/Chris Mars Publishing, Inc. and to Liz Holland. And lastly to the departed masters, you have our eternal respect and are the source of our mutual inspiration. Thank you for being the light in the darkness.

INTRODUCTION

A SEPARATE REALITY. A DARK AND LATENT reality, not accepted by genteel society. An underworld of primordial images and racial memory, an unwanted peek into the darkness of the past, and maybe a glimpse at some not too distant future.

Even today, as man struggles against the beast within, between the light and the darkness in his soul, he sometimes finds that the darkness can be strong, and even the light often verges on shadow, sometimes crossing the boundary to do battle, sometimes winning, sometimes losing to the abyss.

Long before Robin Goodfellow traversed the forests of Shakespeare, the creatures of imagery and form portrayed here were tangible and real. They still exist today.

The Book of Night is about the dark side—our fear of and fascination with the unknown; of things macabre; of things done in secret; of things done in the dark. Death, destruction, loss, pain, these are all within its domain, and if you choose to bear your soul to the night sky and feel its breath, you too will know its mettle, and evoke the images of this separate reality.

Fresh voices and the wisdom of departed masters are both represented for your delight, so please do not hesitate to discover them anew.

Come. The Night awaits

APPARITIONS BY BOB GIADROSICH

CHAPTER 1:

APPARITIONS

STEP INTO THE MIRROR OF MY EYES, AND travel the dark corridors of my mind. The fallen denizens lurking there might give you pause: a siren chained in a brackish moor; a cadaverous fiend with my face frozen in a mirthless grin; the lost youth of hags and mortuary slabs; jack-o-lanterns with all too lifelike fire in their eyes; a small child wandering lost in the ever-present shadows. My apparitions are yours, if only you enter the mist…

DREAM-LAND

Edgar Allan Poe, 1844

BY A ROUTE OBSCURE AND LONELY,
Haunted by ill angels only,
Where an Eidolon, named NIGHT,
On a black throne reigns upright,
I have reached these lands but newly
From an ultimate dim Thule—
From a wild weird clime that lieth, sublime,
Out of SPACE—out of TIME.

Bottomless vales and boundless floods,
And chasms, and caves, and Titian woods,
With forms that no man can discover
For the dews that drip all over;
Mountains toppling evermore
Into seas without a shore;
Seas that restlessly aspire,
Surging, unto skies of fire;
Lakes that endlessly outspread
Their lone waters—lone and dead,—

Their still waters—still and chilly
With the snows of the lolling lily.

By the lakes that thus outspread
Their lone waters, lone and dead,—
Their sad waters, sad and chilly
With the snows of the lolling lily,—
By the mountains—near the river
Murmuring lowly, murmuring ever,—
By the grey woods,—by the swamp
Where the toad and the newt encamp,—
By the dismal tarns and pools
Where dwell the Ghouls,—
By each spot the most unholy—
In each nook most melancholy,—
There the traveller meets aghast
Sheeted Memories of the Past—
Shrouded forms that start and sigh
As they pass the wanderer by—
White-robed forms of friends long given,
In agony, to the Earth—and Heaven.

For the heart whose woes are legion
'Tis a peaceful, soothing region—
For the spirit that walks in shadow
'Tis—oh 'tis an Eldorado!

But the traveller, travelling through it,
May not—dare not openly view it;
Never its mysteries are exposed
To the weak human eye unclosed;
So wills its King, who hath forbid
The uplifting of the fringed lid;
And thus the sad Soul that here passes
Beholds it but through darkened glasses.

By a route obscure and lonely,
Haunted by ill angels only,
Where an Eidolon, named NIGHT,
On a black throne reigns upright,
I have wandered home but newly
From this ultimate dim Thule.

DARKNESS

George Gordon (Lord) Byron, 1816

I HAD A DREAM, WHICH WAS NOT ALL A dream.
The bright sun was extinguish'd, and the stars
Did wander darkling in the eternal space,
Rayless, and pathless, and the icy earth
Swung blind and blackening in the moonless air;
Morn came and went—and came, and brought no
    day,
And men forgot their passions in the dread
Of this their desolation; and all hearts
Were chill'd into a selfish prayer for light:
And they did live by watchfires—and the thrones,
The palaces of crowned kings—the huts,
The habitations of all things which dwell,
Were burnt for beacons; cities were consum'd,
And men were gather'd round their blazing homes
To look once more into each other's face;
Happy were those who dwelt within the eye
Of the volcanos, and their mountain-torch:
A fearful hope was all the world contain'd;

Forests were set on fire—but hour by hour
They fell and faded—and the crackling trunks
Extinguish'd with a crash—and all was black.
The brows of men by the despairing light
Wore an unearthly aspect, as by fits
The flashes fell upon them; some lay down
And hid their eyes and wept; and some did rest
Their chins upon their clenched hands, and smil'd;
And others hurried to and fro, and fed
Their funeral piles with fuel, and look'd up
With mad disquietude on the dull sky,
The pall of a past world; and then again
With curses cast them down upon the dust,
And gnash'd their teeth and howl'd: the wild birds
    shriek'd
And, terrified, did flutter on the ground,
And flap their useless wings; the wildest brutes
Came tame and tremulous; and vipers crawl'd
And twin'd themselves among the multitude,
Hissing, but stingless—they were slain for food.
And War, which for a moment was no more,
Did glut himself again: a meal was bought
With blood, and each sate sullenly apart
Gorging himself in gloom: no love was left;
All earth was but one thought—and that was death
Immediate and inglorious; and the pang

Of famine fed upon all entrails—men
Died, and their bones were tombless as their flesh;
The meagre by the meagre were devour'd,
Even dogs assail'd their masters, all save one,
And he was faithful to a corse, and kept
The birds and beasts and famish'd men at bay,
Till hunger clung them, or the dropping dead
Lur'd their lank jaws; himself sought out no food,
But with a piteous and perpetual moan,
And a quick desolate cry, licking the hand
Which answer'd not with a caress—he died.
The crowd was famish'd by degrees; but two
Of an enormous city did survive,
And they were enemies: they met beside
The dying embers of an altar-place
Where had been heap'd a mass of holy things
For an unholy usage; they rak'd up,
And shivering scrap'd with their cold skeleton hands
The feeble ashes, and their feeble breath
Blew for a little life, and made a flame
Which was a mockery; then they lifted up
Their eyes as it grew lighter, and beheld
Each other's aspects—saw, and shriek'd, and died—
Even of their mutual hideousness they died,
Unknowing who he was upon whose brow
Famine had written Fiend. The world was void,

The populous and the powerful was a lump,

Seasonless, herbless, treeless, manless, lifeless—

A lump of death—a chaos of hard clay.

The rivers, lakes and ocean all stood still,

And nothing stirr'd within their silent depths;

Ships sailorless lay rotting on the sea,

And their masts fell down piecemeal: as they dropp'd

They slept on the abyss without a surge—

The waves were dead; the tides were in their grave,

The moon, their mistress, had expir'd before;

The winds were wither'd in the stagnant air,

And the clouds perish'd; Darkness had no need

Of aid from them—She was the Universe.

THE DEMIURGE'S LAUGH

Robert Frost, 1915

IT WAS FAR IN THE SAMENESS OF THE WOOD;
I was running with joy on the Demon's trail,
Though I knew what I hunted was no true god.
It was just as the light was beginning to fail
That I suddenly heard—all I needed to hear:
It has lasted me many and many a year.
The sound was behind me instead of before,
A sleepy sound, but mocking half,
As of one who utterly couldn't care.
The Demon arose from his wallow to laugh,
Brushing the dirt from his eye as he went;
And well I knew what the Demon meant.
I shall not forget how his laugh rang out.
I felt as a fool to have been so caught,
And checked my steps to make pretence
It was something among the leaves I sought
(Though doubtful whether he stayed to see).
Thereafter I sat me against a tree.

Love's Apparition and Evanishment

Samuel Taylor Coleridge, 1833

IN VAIN I SUPPLICATE THE POWERS ABOVE;
There is no Resurrection for the Love
That, nursed with tenderest care, yet fades away
In the chilled heart by inward self-decay.
Like a lorn Arab old and blind
Some caravan had left behind
That sits beside a ruined Well,
And hangs his wistful head aslant,
Some sound he fain would catch—
Suspended there, as it befell,
O'er my own vacancy,
And while I seemed to watch
The sickly calm, as were of heart
A place where Hope lay dead,
The spirit of departed Love
Stood close beside my bed.
She bent methought to kiss my lips
As she was wont to do.

Alas! 'twas with a chilling breath

That awoke just enough of life in death

To make it die anew.

A VISION OF DOOM

Ambrose Bierce, 1903

I STOOD UPON A HILL. THE SETTING SUN
Was crimson with a curse and a portent,
And scarce his angry ray lit up the land
That lay below, whose lurid gloom appeared
Freaked with a moving mist, which, reeking up
From dim tarns hateful with some horrid ban,
Took shapes forbidden and without a name.
Gigantic night-birds, rising from the reeds
With cries discordant, startled all the air,
And bodiless voices babbled in the gloom—
The ghosts of blasphemies long ages stilled,
And shrieks of women, and men's curses. All
These visible shapes, and sounds no mortal ear
Had ever heard, some spiritual sense
Interpreted, though brokenly; for I
Was haunted by a consciousness of crime,
Some giant guilt, but whose I knew not. All
These things malign, by sight and sound revealed,
Were sin-begotten; that I knew—no more—
And that but dimly, as in dreadful dreams

The sleepy senses babble to the brain
Imperfect witness. As I stood a voice,
But whence it came I knew not, cried aloud
Some words to me in a forgotten tongue,
Yet straight I knew me for a ghost forlorn,
Returned from the illimited inane.
Again, but in a language that I knew,
As in reply to something which in me
Had shaped itself a thought, but found no words,
It spake from the dread mystery about:
"Immortal shadow of a mortal soul
That perished with eternity, attend.
What thou beholdest is as void as thou:
The shadow of a poet's dream—himself
As thou, his soul as thine, long dead,
But not like thine outlasted by its shade.
His dreams alone survive eternity
As pictures in the unsubstantial void.
Excepting thee and me (and we because
The poet wove us in his thought) remains
Of nature and the universe no part
Or vestige but the poet's dreams. This dread,
Unspeakable land about thy feet, with all
Its desolation and its terrors—lo!
'T is but a phantom world. So long ago
That God and all the angels since have died

That poet lived—yourself long dead—his mind
Filled with the light of a prophetic fire,
And standing by the Western sea, above
The youngest, fairest city in the world,
Named in another tongue than his for one
Ensainted, saw its populous domain
Plague-smitten with a nameless shame. For there
Red-handed murder rioted; and there
The people gathered gold, nor cared to loose
The assassin's fingers from the victim's throat,
But said, each in his vile pursuit engrossed:
'Am I my brother's keeper? Let the Law
Look to the matter.' But the Law did not.
And there, O pitiful! the babe was slain
Within its mother's breast and the same grave
Held babe and mother; and the people smiled,
Still gathering gold, and said: 'The Law, the Law,'
Then the great poet, touched upon the lips
With a live coal from Truth's high altar, raised
His arms to heaven and sang a song of doom—
Sang of the time to be, when God should lean
Indignant from the Throne and lift his hand,
And that foul city be no more!—a tale,
A dream, a desolation and a curse!
No vestige of its glory should survive
In fact or memory: its people dead,

Its site forgotten, and its very name
Disputed."
"Was the prophecy fulfilled?"
The sullen disc of the declining sun
Was crimson with a curse and a portent,
And scarce his angry ray lit up the land
That lay below, whose lurid gloom appeared
Freaked with a moving mist, which, reeking up
From dim tarns hateful with a horrid ban,
Took shapes forbidden and without a name.
Gigantic night-birds, rising from the reeds
With cries discordant, startled all the air,
And bodiless voices babbled in the gloom.
But not to me came any voice again;
And, covering my face with thin, dead hands,
I wept, and woke, and cried aloud to God!

PETER'S FIELD
Ralph Waldo Emerson, 1886

[KNOWS HE WHO TILLS THIS LONELY FIELD
To reap its scanty corn,
What mystic fruit his acres yield
At midnight and at morn?]

That field by spirits bad and good,
By Hell and Heaven is haunted,
And every rood in the hemlock wood
I know is ground enchanted.

[In the long sunny afternoon
The plain was full of ghosts:
I wandered up, I wandered down,
Beset by pensive hosts.]

For in those lonely grounds the sun
Shines not as on the town,
In nearer arcs his journeys run,
And nearer stoops the moon.

There in a moment I have seen

The buried Past arise;
The fields of Thessaly grew green,
Old gods forsook the skies.

I cannot publish in my rhyme
What pranks the greenwood played;
It was the Carnival of time,
And Ages went or stayed.

To me that spectral nook appeared
The mustering Day of Doom,
And round me swarmed in shadowy troop
Things past and things to come.

The darkness haunteth me elsewhere;
There I am full of light;
In every whispering leaf I hear
More sense than sages write.

Underwoods were full of pleasance,
All to each in kindness bend,
And every flower made obeisance
As a man unto his friend.

Far seen, the river glides below,
Tossing one sparkle to the eyes:
I catch thy meaning, wizard wave;
The River of my Life replies.

DISAPPEARING

Michael H. Hanson

I THINK I AM DISAPPEARING,
becoming a dim fading flame
drifting in and out of darkness;
a vague mundane will-o'-the-wisp.

Unheeded in workplace hallways.
Ever distant from relatives.
First translucent, then transparent,
light itself invalidates me.

Becoming voice without echo —
breathless shadow; lacking substance.
Will anyone remember me?
I think I am disappearing.

And The Lurker Waits

Richard Groller

NIGHT CRIES.
Callings, deep into the void of night,
somber and terrible and filling the void.

Primordial fear, eclipsing the darkness,
and challenging the infinity of spatial abyss
with cries and shivers and cowering ignorance.

Night cries.

Distant clarions of darker, twilight gods
Cthulhu, Thoth, Samhain, Cernunnos, Hermes, Pan,
calling and chanting them,
promising, tempting them,
heralding them, and summoning them ...

Night cries.

The fires burn bright
to ward off the darkness,
but here at the edge

where the thin veneer
called civilization disappears,
the Lurker waits,
and the Old Ones live once more.

A Fleeting Moment of Remembrance

Jack William Finley

AND JUST LIKE THAT,
the cold, unforgiving breeze
whispers through the trees.

Your house of cards,
so carefully crafted
gone
and with it hope,
fleeting and fragile
slips through your fingers
a fading memory
as if perhaps
it were never really there
at all.

THE RUNNER AT TWILIGHT

Richard Groller

DARK CLOUDS AND AUTUMN TWILIGHT
cool, like the hand of Samhain.
Not the cold dampness of the grave,
but the chilling blade of the stiletto
thrust quickly through the heart,
leaving the victim with inspired visions
of imminent eternity...

Dark clouds overhead billow;
they mask the spirits, formless and malign.
Soul Stealers Life Eaters.
Will-O-The-Wisp by clouds enshrouded,
clothed in night, and hidden
from the unsuspecting eye,
drawing sustenance from the night's offerings...

Autumn sounds and baying hounds;
rustling leaves, their sound retrieves
the memory, of Hellhounds on my heels.

Their eyes ablaze, I know, though I have not seen...

As I run I feel the hot breath behind me,
afraid to turn and face the maw
that rips the flesh and tears with claws
or simply swallows whole...

Twilight time for the poet to write of darkness
and the approaching night. As portals open,
the poet as runner, lopes in hopes of outlasting
the non-light, emerging behind him.

Racing the moon, praying for dawn,
staying ahead of the twilight's spawn,
as the evening's approaching fingers
touch the poet ... the runner stumbles...

The pencil point breaks, writing alone,
as the darkness weaves its web about him,
the poet knows, he is not alone.

PHANTASTIKON

Kurt Newton

THIS DOPPELGANGER
from time past
that appears to me,
that mirrors me

This interloper —
distant, fleeting,
yet near enough for
fear to reach

This phantastikon —
this reverie;
this inner spell toward
which I'm drawn

This apparition —
this ghostly witness
that speaks of visions
from beyond

FOLLOW ME BY PAUL BIELACZYC

From "The Death of Halpin Frayser"

Ambrose Bierce, 1891

'ENTHRALLED BY SOME MYSTERIOUS
spell, I stood
In the lit gloom of an enchanted wood.
The cypress there and myrtle twined their boughs,
Significant, in baleful brotherhood.
'The brooding willow whispered to the yew;
Beneath, the deadly nightshade and the rue,
With immortelles self-woven into strange
Funereal shapes, and horrid nettles grew.
'No song of bird nor any drone of bees,
Nor light leaf lifted by the wholesome breeze:
The air was stagnant all, and Silence was
A living thing that breathed among the trees.
'Conspiring spirits whispered in the gloom,
Half-heard, the stilly secrets of the tomb.
With blood the trees were all adrip; the leaves
Shone in the witch-light with a ruddy bloom.
'I cried aloud! — the spell, unbroken still,

Rested upon my spirit and my will.

Unsouled, unhearted, hopeless and forlorn,

I strove with monstrous presages of ill!

BEYOND THE BLUE VEIL

Kurt Newton

ON OUR MAIDEN VOYAGE ACROSS THE sea,
we witnessed a strange blue apparition
where none should be,
a curtain of rain, we thought, or wall of mist, of a
    color both rich and pale
that a crew member named the blue veil.

But as we approached, our curiosity piqued,
the air turned cold and clouds formed dark and bleak.
A storm took hold and tossed us like a barnacle on
    the back of an angry whale,
and we lost sight of the blue veil.

The crew held on day and night with little sleep,
fighting wind and rain and mammoth waves with
    white foam peaks.
Just when it appeared our names would become part
    of some sad sea-faring tale,
we reached the calm beyond the blue veil.

Such ominous beauty yawned before us as we stood
    upon the deck,
a verdant land as lush and long as any fertile coastal
    neck
sat upon the ocean calm as if gifted by the Gods for
    our travails,
for having gone beyond the blue veil.

But God's gifts can sometimes be not what one
    expects.
When half the crew boarded a skiff and rowed to
    shore, they were promptly met
by a naked tribe of hominids waving frantically as if
    to warn us to turn back and set our sails,
to take us back before we tacked beyond the blue veil.

The instant our crew set foot upon the beach's head,
they began to grunt and drool, their arms hung low,
    their statures bent,
like the native hominids they too waved their arms
    and beseeched us with their primitive wails
for us to leave this strange lagoon for the blue veil.
With half our crew now lost to some unknown
    regressive trait,
we raised sail and caught a breeze that took us from
    the reef into the ocean waves,

back to the very spot where we fought for our lives
    against the pelting rain and blowing gales,
back to, back through, the waiting aqua haze of the
    blue veil.

Back forward into time we swept, from blue into the
    grey,
back into the blackened storm that, before, had
    nearly sent us to our graves,
our skeleton crew performed as admirably as any the
    sea had ever seen set sail,
as we mourned our loss and moved beyond the blue
    veil.

Now many a nautical mile separate us from the
    incident of that day,
but a distressing and most vile condition has gripped
    the men that still remain,
their sudden brutish behavior has me exiled in my
    cabin, with physical changes on every scale,
cursing all the while the day we voyaged beyond the
    blue veil.

THE SHADE

Lori Martin

IN AN OLD TRUNK, SMELLING OF ROTTING
clothes
I found a small book
Kept by father to remind him of what had made him

He was out by the corn growing through the back
forty
When he saw the old man: pale and thin
In loose overalls and a straw hat
Close to the creek, in the shade

Daddy went closer to ask him if he needed help
More to find out what he was doing there
And written in a small cramped hand, my daddy
wrote
"I stepped closer and the hairs on my neck stood up"

And mine did too.

My father had stopped well before he reached him
The man smiled and his frail form vanished

as if he'd never been there
Another treasure, a box of photos
kept here to keep my mother from crying
The last one, taken when the black masses within
  him had nearly won
The last time he'd be out to the back forty

Chemo had taken his teddy bear frame; radiation his
  color
And even though he couldn't feed himself
He still smiled for the camera, from the shade
In loose overalls and a straw hat.

EN-DOR

Rudyard Kipling, 1919

*Behold there is a woman that hath
a familiar spirit at En-dor.*

1 Samuel xxviii 7

THE ROAD TO EN-DOR IS EASY TO TREAD
For Mother or yearning Wife.
There, it is sure, we shall meet our Dead
As they were even in life.
Earth has not dreamed of the blessing in store
For desolate hearts on the road to En-dor.
Whispers shall comfort us out of the dark—
Hands—ah God!—that we knew!
Visions and voices—look and hark!—
Shall prove that the tale is true,
And that those who have passed to the further shore
May be hailed—at a price—on the road to En-dor.

But they are so deep in their new eclipse
Nothing they say can reach,
Unless it be uttered by alien lips
And framed in a stranger's speech.

The son must send word to the mother that bore,
Through an hireling's mouth. 'Tis the rule of En-dor.

And not for nothing these gifts are shown
By such as delight our dead.
They must twitch and stiffen and slaver and groan
Ere the eyes are set in the head,
And the voice from the belly begins. Therefore,
We pay them a wage where they ply at En-dor.

Even so, we have need off faith
And patience to follow the clue.
Often, at first, what the dear one saith
Is babble, or jest, or untrue.
(Lying spirits perplex us sore
Till our loves—and their lives—are well-known at
        En-dor . . . .

Oh the road to En-dor is the oldest road
And the craziest road of all!
Straight it runs to the Witch's abode,
As it did in the days of Saul,
And nothing has changed of the sorrow in store
For such as go down on the road to En-dor!

THE CALL

Rupert Brooke, 1915

OUT OF THE NOTHINGNESS OF SLEEP,
The slow dreams of Eternity,
There was a thunder on the deep:
I came, because you called to me.

I broke the Night's primeval bars,
I dared the old abysmal curse,
And flashed through ranks of frightened stars
Suddenly on the universe!

The eternal silences were broken;
Hell became Heaven as I passed. —
What shall I give you as a token,
A sign that we have met, at last?

I'll break and forge the stars anew,
Shatter the heavens with a song;
Immortal in my love for you,
Because I love you, very strong.

Your mouth shall mock the old and wise,
Your laugh shall fill the world with flame,
I'll write upon the shrinking skies
The scarlet splendour of your name,

Till Heaven cracks, and Hell thereunder
Dies in her ultimate mad fire,
And darkness falls, with scornful thunder,
On dreams of men and men's desire.

Then only in the empty spaces,
Death, walking very silently,
Shall fear the glory of our faces
Through all the dark infinity.

So, clothed about with perfect love,
The eternal end shall find us one,
Alone above the Night, above
The dust of the dead gods, alone.

THE NIGHTMARE

Jillian A. Perkins

VAMPIRES QUENCH THEIR UNDYING
thirsts
With blessings from Cain's unholy curse
Endless rapes from immortals lusts
Brings forth lovers that will never trust

Undead heroes lie in their graves
Waiting an eternity to be saved
Werewolves stalk and roam the Earth
Bringing us to our beds of dirt

Kill the sun, burn down the sky
Death is sweet and so am I
Live tomorrow, leave today
Anarchy has come to stay

Drink the fire and live again
This paradise will never end
Darkness reigns with genocide
Everyone's committing suicide

Your hell, is my heaven
Full of sin, the deadly seven
Follow me you'll live forever
Join me now, it's now or never

THE SHADOW PEOPLE BY BOB GIADROSICH

THE SHADOW PEOPLE

Larry Atchley, Jr.

I SEE THE SHADOW PEOPLE
Out of the corner of my eye
Cloaked in darkness
Enshrouded in secrets
My mind they can't deny

Harbingers of dread and fear
Are they here to help or harm?
Benevolent spirits
Or malevolent entities
My senses reeling with alarm

Appearing to me often
Messengers of death
Their silent dance
And eerie skulking
Nearly take my breath
They forewarn of change
Whether fair or ill

Heralds of destiny
In my mind and in my eyes
Haunting me still

OPHELIA IN DREAMS

Kimberly Richardson

I LOOK UPON HER DEAD FACE-
Finally, she is at peace.
Her limbs stretched out gracefully
Her blood
Creating a crown;
Queen of Darkness and Death.
So I worship eagerly;
Her eyes,
Black dead eyes
Staring beyond
To her final destination
I know not.
But her face
Not a grimace
Only thoughts.
She, thanking me
On her last decaying breath.

THE BELLS

Edgar Allan Poe, 1849

I

HEAR THE SLEDGES WITH THE BELLS—
Silver bells!
What a world of merriment their melody
foretells!
How they tinkle, tinkle, tinkle,
In their icy air of night!
While the stars, that oversprinkle
All the heavens, seem to twinkle
With a crystalline delight;
Keeping time, time, time,
In a sort of Runic rhyme,
To the tintinnabulation that so musically wells
From the bells, bells, bells, bells,
Bells, bells, bells—
From the jingling and the tinkling of the bells.

II

HEAR THE MELLOW WEDDING BELLS,
    Golden bells!
    What a world of happiness their harmony
foretells!
Through the balmy air of night
How they ring out their delight!
From the molten golden-notes,
And all in tune,
What a liquid ditty floats
To the turtle-dove that listens, while she gloats
On the moon!
Oh, from out the sounding cells,
What a gush of euphony voluminously wells!
How it swells!
How it dwells
On the future! how it tells
Of the rapture that impels
To the swinging and the ringing
Of the bells, bells, bells,
Of the bells, bells, bells, bells,
Bells, bells, bells—
To the rhyming and the chiming of the bells!

III

HEAR THE LOUD ALARUM BELLS—
Brazen bells!
What a tale of terror now their turbulency tells!
In the startled ear of night
How they scream out their affright!
Too much horrified to speak,
They can only shriek, shriek,
Out of tune,
In a clamorous appealing to the mercy of the fire,
In a mad expostulation with the deaf and frantic fire
Leaping higher, higher, higher,
With a desperate desire,
And a resolute endeavor
Now—now to sit or never,
By the side of the pale-faced moon.
Oh, the bells, bells, bells!
What a tale their terror tells
Of Despair!
How they clang, and clash, and roar!
What a horror they outpour
On the bosom of the palpitating air!
Yet the ear it fully knows,
By the twanging,
And the clanging,
How the danger ebbs and flows;

Yet the ear distinctly tells,

In the jangling,

And the wrangling,

How the danger sinks and swells,

By the sinking or the swelling in the anger of the
bells—

Of the bells—

Of the bells, bells, bells, bells,

Bells, bells, bells—

In the clamor and the clangor of the bells!

IV

HEAR THE TOLLING OF THE BELLS —
Iron bells!
What a world of solemn thought their monody
compels!

In the silence of the night,

How we shiver with affright

At the melancholy menace of their tone!

For every sound that floats

From the rust within their throats

Is a groan.

And the people—ah, the people—

They that dwell up in the steeple.

All alone,

And who toiling, toiling, toiling,

In that muffled monotone,
Feel a glory in so rolling
On the human heart a stone—
They are neither man nor woman—
They are neither brute nor human —
They are Ghouls:
And their king it is who tolls;
And he rolls, rolls, rolls,
Rolls
A pæan from the bells!
And his merry bosom swells
With the pæan of the bells!
And he dances, and he yells;
Keeping time, time, time,
In a sort of Runic rhyme,
To the pæan of the bells —
Of the bells:
Keeping time, time, time,
In a sort of Runic rhyme,
To the throbbing of the bells —
Of the bells, bells, bells —
To the sobbing of the bells;
Keeping time, time, time,
As he knells, knells, knells,
In a happy Runic rhyme,
To the rolling of the bells—

Of the bells, bells, bells-
To the tolling of the bells,
Of the bells, bells, bells, bells,
Bells, bells, bells —
To the moaning and the groaning of the bells.

NIGHTMARE JESUS

Bill Snider

NIGHTMARE JESUS WEEPS FOR YOU.
For your pain, your misery, your woe.
He sleeps amongst the cemetery roses
Waiting for you to return to the living.

The world
The windows we look through
The eyes
The soul of life that spirits us past
The future
The escape writ upon pages vast
The word
The concepts running past our lives
The silence
The comforting sense of limitless space
The dark
The colour of being both live and dead
The doubts
The everyday commonplace issues
The thoughts

The time we spend in boxes and bags
The images
The miasma that we fixate upon each day
The dreams
The leavings that we clutter our minds with
The end

Nightmare Jesus knows your dreams and nightmares;
He reaches into each one and rearranges them.
Putting everything into context, thought and fiddle
Features and palimpsests present and accounted for.
We are the images
That we make of the world
We are the eyes
That watch over the children
We are the thoughts
That both save and damn the living
We are the terrors
That strike fear amongst the survivors
We are the wonders
That keep society burning
We are the fires
That shadow the concepts buried deep
We are the future
That nebulous gloaming that's always foaming
We are the choices

That spritz the present with tide and prescience
We are the peace
That the savage beast seeks in mirrors and bright
We are the feast
That all creatures want, even though they lack
We are the end.

Nightmare Jesus, weeps out your dreams and
    nightmares
Even after all that he's shared, your pain he no longer
    cares.
The end is coming, he's clear and near to that which
    will occur
Might as well get used to it, as he's also the only one
    with a cure.

AD AGE

Michael H. Hanson

SPEEDY ALKA-SELTZER REALLY GREW UP
but he didn't get fragged in Viet Nam
or croak from mainlining agent orange.
Asthmatic fuck sells Amway in Utah.

The Oscar Meyer Kid craved attention,
matured fat with acne, read comic books,
and outdid John Wayne Gacy's body count.
Shiv'd in ADX Supermax shower.

Quisp did not become a sideshow carny —
doesn't reside in New Jersey Barrens.
Lost, hitching, near Area Fifty One
he's "The Thing" on Route Ten, Arizona.

Ronald McDonald was an albino,
replaced and deported in 2003,
joined Al Qaeda, wounded, nabbed in '04.
Paints Riq'a art with feces at Gitmo.

THE MECHANICS OF EVIL

Dean M. Drinkel

NO RESPITE FROM THE BARRAGE OF
insults.
Deserted among the streets of Paris.
The gothic architecture offers scant protection.
A lost muse, hanging around Rue Bellot,
Waiting for a glimpse of the golden angel.

A knife drawn from its scabbard, silver
Glints in twilight, its teeth are hungry, desires
To feast. Please don't come, not now, not never.
I fear what you will become. The dream transformed
Into a nightmare.

In the shadows, a dog barks. I run my tongue over
Freshly painted graffiti sprayed upon a street sign.
The cafe where I sit is buzzing heaving, the stench of
Rotting flesh all around me. Forgive us Lord, we
    know
Full well what we do. My fingers tighten around the
    handle,

The blade longs to caress your skin. A scarlet kiss
    awaits.

Then when I have given up all hope of salvation, I go
    to leave,
Happy our paths did not cross. Your life has been
    saved,
If only from a dark memory. But when I turn around,
You stand there smiling, I wave and say hello,
Let the metal in my hand do all the talking.
I am deafened to your screams.

LAZARUS RISING

Dean M. Drinkel

OO SOON THE YEARNING, WITH IT
comes
The scream. The young and old cry in
Unison. Nature, drunk on its own
Apathy reaches for reason. Gone though
Too and how we mock when it drowns
In self pity.

Ploughed fields offer new hope in
Its furrows. Messages from hell,
Warning of the new danger everywhere.
The torch song of our own mothers.
A beacon through the night. Yet,
Turn away we must.
Golden visions un-weave. Spreading
Poison through the realm. Bled into us,
Convince others we're alive. Forbid it!
Hide in the elements, we are the
Children of the new dawn. Father,
Forgive them.

JAPANESE GARDEN

Angel Weaver

SHADES OF US PAINTED GREEN CANVAS
as the sun warmed the stone bench
where we sat in the velvet silence of
cherry blossom petals on the breeze –
a perfumed world, disarmingly perfect.
The descending sun made us golden,
and the last rays on the koi pond
illuminated the metallic flash of fins
as fish swam in dizzying circles –
a slow circuit, then faster and faster.
As the sky darkened, I turned to you.
You were there, and you were gone -
shriveled blossoms falling one by one.
At water's edge I saw you as though
through a glass, dirty and dark –
your dim reflection on the surface
at odds with all that you were –
skin too pale, eyes darkened, and lips
moving with words I could not hear.
My trembling hand reached out to you -

seeking fingers touched only cool water
where I thought our skin should meet.
Ripples fanned out, disturbing your image –
when the water cleared, you were gone.

THE DANCE OF DEATH

Johann Wolfgang von Goethe, 1813

Translation by Edgar A. Bowring, 1853

THE WARDER LOOKS DOWN AT THE MID
hour of night,
   On the tombs that lie scatter'd below:
The moon fills the place with her silvery light,

And the churchyard like day seems to glow.
When see! first one grave, then another opes wide,
And women and men stepping forth are descried,

In cerements snow-white and trailing.

In haste for the sport soon their ankles they twitch,

And whirl round in dances so gay;

The young and the old, and the poor, and the rich,

But the cerements stand in their way;
And as modesty cannot avail them aught here,
They shake themselves all, and the shrouds soon
    appear
Scatter'd over the tombs in confusion.

Now waggles the leg, and now wriggles the thigh,

As the troop with strange gestures advance,
And a rattle and clatter anon rises high,

As of one beating time to the dance.
The sight to the warder seems wondrously queer,
When the villainous Tempter speaks thus in his ear:

"Seize one of the shrouds that lie yonder!"

Quick as thought it was done! and for safety he fled

Behind the church-door with all speed;
The moon still continues her clear light to shed

On the dance that they fearfully lead.
But the dancers at length disappear one by one,
And their shrouds, ere they vanish, they carefully don,

And under the turf all is quiet.

But one of them stumbles and shuffles there still,

And gropes at the graves in despair;
Yet 'tis by no comrade he's treated so ill

The shroud he soon scents in the air.
So he rattles the door—for the warder 'tis well
That 'tis bless'd, and so able the foe to repel,

All cover'd with crosses in metal.

The shroud he must have, and no rest will allow,

There remains for reflection no time;
On the ornaments Gothic the wight seizes now,

And from point on to point hastes to climb.
Alas for the warder! his doom is decreed!
Like a long-legged spider, with ne'er-changing speed,

Advances the dreaded pursuer.

The warder he quakes, and the warder turns pale,

The shroud to restore fain had sought;
When the end,—now can nothing to save him avail,—

In a tooth formed of iron is caught.
With vanishing lustre the moon's race is run,
When the bell thunders loudly a powerful One,

And the skeleton fails, crush'd to atoms.

AUTUMN PEOPLE BY BOB GIADROSICH

CHAPTER 2:

AUTUMN PEOPLE

AUTUMN. THE DARKLY SWEET REALM born between the equinox and the solstice, preparing for Yule, and enjoying the harvest before winter's cold crush.

Autumn. The time of All Hallows, of hooded sky and primal colors, presaging pristine death in the season of the Fall.

Autumn. Time to wink at macabre pumpkins that glare back in garish grimness. And time to renew acquaintance with the wistful moon and Samhain.

Come. Join me and seek solace among our like minded kindred, the autumn people...

Come. The Night awaits.

ULALUME

Edgar Allan Poe, 1847

THE SKIES THEY WERE ASHEN AND SOBER;
The leaves they were crisped and sere—
The leaves they were withering and sere;
It was night in the lonesome October
Of my most immemorial year:
It was hard by the dim lake of Auber,
In the misty mid region of Weir:—
It was down by the dank tarn of Auber,
In the ghoul-haunted woodland of Weir.

Here once, through an alley Titanic,
Of cypress, I roamed with my Soul—
Of cypress, with Psyche, my Soul.
There were days when my heart was volcanic
As the scoriac rivers that roll—
As the lavas that restlessly roll
Their sulphurous currents down Yaanek,
In the ultimate climes of the Pole—
That groan as they roll down Mount Yaanek
In the realms of the Boreal Pole.

Our talk had been serious and sober,
But our thoughts they were palsied and sere—
Our memories were treacherous and sere;
For we knew not the month was October,
And we marked not the night of the year—
(Ah, night of all nights in the year!)
We noted not the dim lake of Auber,
(Though once we had journeyed down here)
We remembered not the dank tarn of Auber,
Nor the ghoul-haunted woodland of Weir.

And now, as the night was senescent,
And star-dials pointed to morn—
As the star-dials hinted of morn—
At the end of our path a liquescent
And nebulous lustre was born,
Out of which a miraculous crescent
Arose with a duplicate horn—
Astarte's bediamonded crescent,
Distinct with its duplicate horn.

And I said—"She is warmer than Dian:
She rolls through an ether of sighs—
She revels in a region of sighs.
She has seen that the tears are not dry on
These cheeks, where the worm never dies,

And has come past the stars of the Lion,
To point us the path to the skies—
To the Lethean peace of the skies—
Come up, in despite of the Lion,
To shine on us with her bright eyes—
Come up, through the lair of the Lion,
With love in her luminous eyes."

But Psyche, uplifting her finger,
Said—"Sadly this star I mistrust—
Her pallor I strangely mistrust—
Ah, hasten!—ah, let us not linger!
Ah, fly!—let us fly!—for we must."
In terror she spoke; letting sink her
Wings till they trailed in the dust—
In agony sobbed, letting sink her
Plumes till they trailed in the dust—
Till they sorrowfully trailed in the dust.

I replied—"This is nothing but dreaming.
Let us on, by this tremulous light!
Let us bathe in this crystalline light!
Its Sybillic splendor is beaming
With Hope and in Beauty to-night—
See!—it flickers up the sky through the night!
Ah, we safely may trust to its gleaming,
And be sure it will lead us aright—

We safely may trust to a gleaming
That cannot but guide us aright,
Since it flickers up to Heaven through the night."

Thus I pacified Psyche and kissed her,
And tempted her out of her gloom—
And conquered her scruples and gloom;
And we passed to the end of the vista—
But were stopped by the door of a tomb—
By the door of a legended tomb:—
And I said—"What is written, sweet sister,
On the door of this legended tomb?"
She replied—"Ulalume—Ulalume—
'T is the vault of thy lost Ulalume!"

Then my heart it grew ashen and sober
As the leaves that were crisped and sere—
As the leaves that were withering and sere—
And I cried—"It was surely October
On this very night of last year,
That I journeyed—I journeyed down here!—
That I brought a dread burden down here—
On this night, of all nights in the year,
Ah, what demon has tempted me here?
Well I know, now, this dim lake of Auber—
This misty mid region of Weir:—

Well I know, now, this dank tarn of Auber—
This ghoul-haunted woodland of Weir."

A PEN AND A PROMISE TO KEEP

Kurt Newton

EDGAR, DEAR EDGAR, YOU HAVE UNFAIRLY
Drawn the task too tall to meet,
Giving us such dark visions it barely
Allows my pen one sentence complete.

Rest assured I will not tire, however,
Attempt as I might, I know I will never
Leave as great a mark as you have done,
Let me at least achieve a smaller one?

Allow me this and I will offer my soul,
Nevermore will your tales be unheard.
Poetry will rise and I'll act out the role,
Only you will provide every word.
Edgar, dear Edgar, I give you my word.

THE RAKING MAN

Michael H. Hanson

PRAY DO NOT FEAR THIS WORKING MAN
who gathers leaves by sturdy hand.
My rakish grin and cotton gloves
are harbingers of autumn love.

Mysterious, misunderstood
I haunt each musky neighborhood.
With wistful eyes of hazel green
I saunter through your lusty dreams.

Arcane protector of your yard,
I am sweet nature's loamy bard.
Most favored son of mother earth
I sing of ritual rebirth.

I dare not tarry very long,
far from the forest's eldritch song;
and mimicking last winter's bier,
I burrow down until next year.

Bad Day At The Beach

Bill Snider

THIS MORNING, I AWOKE AND WENT TO
the beach.
   It was a beautiful day; the sun shone brightly,
The waves lapped gently against the sand.
I could see for miles past the lighthouse
The air was fresh and brimming with promise.

I took my time to gather my wits for the day
Spending time with my girls and their quirks
I cooked them breakfast, and made jokes
It was all that I could do to contain myself
Knowing how much that I loved them.
We spent the remainder of that morning
Quaintly involved in the simple art of wander.
Up and down the beach, stopping intermittently
To play with something lost or found in the sand.
My girls giggled, I laughed; time well expended.

I walked deeper into the surf, my legs encased
By the cool lap of the waves from the ocean.

It's touch sent shocking shivers up my spine
And I relaxed to the soft rhythm of its embrace.
I looked back to see my girls still playing in the sand.

Without warning, though, I was wakened to a noise
Vicious, violent; something bestial, out of place.
Two men came running from down the coastline
They scrambled at a pace I could not believe
As they ran past where my girls last I did spy.

I shouted as loud as I could, as I witnessed horror.
These strangers leapt upon my daughters, my wife
Ripped and torn, rag dolls tossed into the sand.
I stood in shock, rooted to the spot that I was at.
The surf continued to pull at me, out to the ocean.

I could not move, as the monsters finished their meal
My girls, so full of life and frailties, nothing anymore.
The monsters seemed not to notice me, in the waters
As if my presence there was completely invisible to
    them.
I wanted to scream and holler and shake my fists!

But I knew better as a cold part of me fell into place.
I paused, letting them move on past this sandy beach;
And I followed them, quietly, like a shadow's breath.
On the way towards my lighthouse they moved

The only other place of human habitation here.

Along the way, I picked up a shovel from the sand
Something wicked, and heavy, and sharply tanned.
With cold and calculating eyes I watched them scurry
As they scuttled closer to my now empty homestead.
Where my girls had played for the entirety of their
    lives.

A tear escaped my eye with that lonesome thought
And in the next moment I partook of my actions
    fully.
There were but two of the vile villains in that midst
With wide, quick slices of the shovel in my hands
I soon parted their heads from the bloodied bodies.

A stench most foul arose from their carcasses in that
    sand
To my knees I did fall, while I replayed those
    moments again.
I steeled myself, to clean up what had been wrought.
The monsters were burned and my girls were
    gathered
As much as could possible be under the
    circumstances.

I buried what remained of them in the garden she
    kept
A quiet little space sheltered from the waves and
    storms.
Her place of solace, she'd always said often at times.
And now my girls final resting place for all eternity.
Again, upon completing this work, I cried upon my
    knees.

This day, that started full of promise, of joy, of
    wonder
Burned into ruin and ashes and blasphemous murder.
And thus, I am now found, wandering the roads back
To civilization, or as much of it that humanity could
    muster.
Broken cities and barren landscapes are all that I find.

The news, the last bit that I could find proclaimed
Quite clear, quite brazen for all that could read
It was the end of the world, who could doubt?
Certainly, not I, as my world had already finished
Upon the island of my birth, my lighthouse, now
    forgot.

MY NOVEMBER GUEST

Robert Frost, 1915

MY SORROW, WHEN SHE'S HERE WITH ME,
Thinks these dark days of autumn rain
Are beautiful as days can be;
She loves the bare, the withered tree;
She walks the sodden pasture lane.

Her pleasure will not let me stay.
She talks and I am fain to list:
She's glad the birds are gone away,
She's glad her simple worsted gray
Is silver now with clinging mist.

The desolate, deserted trees,
The faded earth, the heavy sky,
The beauties she so truly sees,
She thinks I have no eye for these,
And vexes me for reason why.

Not yesterday I learned to know
The love of bare November days
Before the coming of the snow,
But it were vain to tell her so,
And they are better for her praise.

MOON ON TREE TOP BY LIZ HOLLAND

SONNET: TO THE AUTUMNAL MOON

Samuel Taylor Coleridge, 1788

MILD SPLENDOUR OF THE VARIOUS-
vested Night!
Mother of wildly-working visions! hail!
I watch thy gliding, while with watery light
Thy weak eye glimmers through a fleecy veil;
And when thou lovest thy pale orb to shroud
Behind the gather'd blackness lost on high;
And when thou dartest from the wind-rent cloud
Thy placid lightning o'er the awaken'd sky.

Ah such is Hope! as changeful and as fair!
Now dimly peering on the wistful sight;
Now hid behind the dragon-wing'd Despair:
But soon emerging in her radiant might
She o'er the sorrow-clouded breast of Care
Sails, like a meteor kindling in its flight.

CONSTANCY

Ambrose Bierce, 1903

DULL WERE THE DAYS AND SOBER,
The mountains were brown and bare,
For the season was sad October
And a dirge was in the air.
The mated starlings flew over
To the isles of the southern sea.
She wept for her warrior lover—
Wept and exclaimed: "Ah, me!

"Long years have I mourned my darling
In his battle-bed at rest;
And it's O, to be a starling,
With a mate to share my nest!"
The angels pitied her sorrow,
Restoring her warrior's life;
And he came to her arms on the morrow
To claim her and take her to wife.
An aged lover—a portly,
Bald lover, a trifle too stiff,
With manners that would have been courtly,
And would have been graceful, if—

If the angels had only restored him
Without the additional years
That had passed since the enemy bored him
To death with their long, sharp spears.
As it was, he bored her, and she rambled
Away with her father's young groom,
And the old lover smiled as he ambled
Contentedly back to the tomb.

Stalker

Michael H. Hanson

YOU FOLLOW ME,
yet not so near,
keeping distance,
but surrendering no space,
at constant pace
with my every doubt;
uncaring companion,
relentless hound.

I cannot flee.
There's no true escape
from that which has no substance
and will not show its harsh face,
that inner hidden mask
of night sweats,
heart pains,
and lonely panic.

You yearn to drag me
down, flailing, helpless,

at odds with joy,
and hope, and passion,
most ghastly brain-worm
savagely gnawing.
Despair, I name you,
but cannot cast you out.

THE EDITOR'S LAMENT

Allan Gilbreath

HERE I SIT IN MY OFFICE, DARK AND
dreary.
My eyes are tired, my body weary.
I am looking over the unopened pile.
I shake my head and moan for a while.

Every editor is accused of being a hideous beast,
of being callous and hard, not caring the least,
with reptilian scales and horns most large.
I must confess to being guilty of this charge.

Before you scorn me and turn away,
I pray that you will listen to what I have to say.
I was once human, just like you,
but I was changed by this mutagenic poetic goo.

Do not laugh or scoff or say untrue
unless you want my fate to befall you.
It all began so innocently early one morning.
Edit these I was asked, without any warning.

I leapt to the task. I took the bait.
How was I to know my monstrous fate?
What treasures awaited me I could only hope
as I opened that first fateful envelope.

Her unrequited love made her wish to die
by thrusting hot needles in her eye.
I knew how she felt, her words so correct.
Reading her poem had much the same effect.

The next piece was about a lover's heart being
    untrue.
The lover should make her his wife or be made into
    glue.
I checked the age of this writer but not a wife.
Geez kid, you're fourteen. Get a life!

At this point, I did not understand
that my fate was being shaped by so cruel a hand.
The more I read, the thicker my skin did grow,
by the second day, the horns had begun to show.

The next poet was an angry young man,
he wrote he was tattooed and avoided a tan
to protest his displeasure with the world.

I assured him his work was not set aside, it was
   hurled.

Then came a mind numbing epic saga of everyman's
   life.
This guy did nothing for 90 pages, no happiness, no
   strife.
The saga just lay there with nothing to read.
I suggested the author be fixed before he could breed.

I was not too far-gone for salvation
but this literary punishment was beyond
   contemplation.
My fangs began to grow long and white.
My eyes even began glowing red at night.

An effort labeled erotic was the very next treat.
It was written in lipstick on a torn piece of bed sheet.
My answer was, "Oh, I wish to see even simple
   poetic devices
but thank you for the tour of your strange perverted
   vices!"

The next 20 works were all staring at the moon.
Lovers were dropping like flies, all in an impassioned
   swoon.
I neatly stacked the entire batch
and laughed hysterically as I found a match.

The horns looked good and the scales were bright.
Everyone knew I was an editor on sight.
My transformation was nearly complete
but my heart was not completely concrete.

The next 300 were all odes to pets.
I chose one about a cat by a woman named Getz.
I sent an invitation to meet this interesting cat.
How do you like my cute fuzzy new hat?

The final blow was finally struck.
The 40,000 teenage angst poems hit like a truck.
So much whining, complaining and cussing all before
    life has really begun,
now I know why tigers eat their young.

If you wish to avoid my horrible wrath when you
    write.
Let me show you how. Let me show you the light.
Give your work soul. Give your work heart.
Trying looking up the words before you start.

If you wish to avoid my monstrous fate
practice your craft, learn to create
and if asked to edit just a little, do not be swayed.
Run my friends and be very very afraid.

Faerie Fire

Richard Groller

FAERIE FIRE, BRIGHT CORONA
bathe the Earth in muted light
Elvenfire, rainbow prisms
lurking minions rule the night.

Who befriends me? Child of Darkness
Moon is full, it calls tonight
lunar temptress, Child of Darkness
dance with glee at Hell's delight.

Joyous laughter, wild abandon
Rites of Bacchus stir the night
Faerie fire fills the night sky
Child of Darkness, rue the Light.

FAERIE FIRE BY MICHAEL BIELACZYC

DREAMER

Jack William Finley

I AM THE MAN IN THE SHADOWS.
The man who watches the men behind the curtain,
unseen voyeur
watching,
listening,
waiting…
I am the sound at the heart of the silence
Both near
And impossibly far away
The whisper on the wind
The seed of life
The answer to the questions you are afraid to ask
Both the dreamer
And the dream
Do you
Can you
IMAGINE
Are YOU
The dreamer
Or the dreamed

Am I dreaming you
Or are YOU
Dreaming me?

BELOVED DARKNESS

Richard Groller

GREY ARE THE AUTUMN TREES, BY
winter's onset
robbbed of their leaves
Greens, reds and golds, and crispy cold
partake of loving sleep, of winter's gentle death....

A time of cool breezes, collars turned to the cold,
turtlenecks and pullovers and hot mulled cider;
rolling hills and fertile knolls, by frost bereft of
their summer glory. The trees seem lifeless as death,
yet they feel my soul, they know my sorrow...

Nights enchanted allure, accursed love, beloved
　　darkness
my sweet cherished shadow comes to me only in the
　　twilight, only in the season of dark tide.
Dim to sight, cool to touch, yet warm to my heart
ever to share my side, but never to join, she steals my
　　heart.
In the dark of night, under overcast twilight, is

the Other Side. The umbra of my better self, my
    better half.
Accursed love beloved darkness,
an image ever veiled in night
Nightshade, Beguiling Shade, Shade of Autumn,
Accursed love beloved darkness in my heart.

MURDER'S CALL BY PAUL BIELACZYC

THE CROWS OF LAS CRUCES REVISITED

Kurt Newton

I

THE CROWS OF LAS CRUCES
descended in flocks
of thousands or more,
settling blackly, thickly
upon the rocks,
and dry dust desert floor.

At first no thought
was given twice,
for stranger things have flown
in on the desert wind
to stay the night
and rest their bones.

"They're here to raise the dead,"
the old Indian woman said,
sitting at her roadside stand,

painting crows on smooth round stones
with blinded-eye and crippled-hand.

With summer past
the nights grew long,
each one blacker than before.
The townspeople waited
for the crows to move on,
but in flew several thousand more.

And though they flooded
the streets in town
and perched in curtains on the eaves,
it was the cemetery where
they eventually touched down,
the place, it is said, where no one leaves.

"They're here to make the dead alive,"
the old Indian woman cried,
sitting at her roadside stand,
weaving strings into bird-like things
with blinded-eye and crippled-hand.

But no one paid
the old woman heed,
for the dead had never slipped
out from beneath
the desert scrub and weed

or breached a family crypt.

And so it was
on All Hallow's Eve,
the crows began to stretch their wings.
While children, dressed
in make believe,
collected candy-coated things.

"The dead are coming home,"
the old Indian woman was heard to groan,
before closing up her roadside stand,
a talisman for each child's grin
with curious-eye and outstretched-hand.

One by one, into
the starlit night,
to the edge of town the children were led
their spirits strong,
their energy bright,
to the cemetery to jumpstart the dead.

But as the children descended
upon the graveyard stones,
the crows of Las Cruces had fled.
In their place were the old
Indian woman's bones

and a note in the sand that read:

"Go home, young ones, to sleep,
I have given the dead my soul to keep.
But the gifts I gave to you will bind.
Remember me on All Hallow's Eve,
for when your breath leaves, your soul is mine."

H

NOW FIFTY YEARS
have come and gone,
the children flown
to every corner of
the country and beyond
to lead lives of their own.

But in their dreams
they often hear,
as if without a choice,
a plaintive whisper
in their ear
of an old Indian woman's voice.

"Your time is setting like the sun.
Your soul is mine, my little one."
And in each dream a crow appears

with oily wings and eyes of ink
to wake them in a grip of fear.

The talismans sat
on tables and shelves,
a keepsake they couldn't lose.
The children, now grown,
had forgotten the spell
that bound them in their youth.

But one by one,
as their death drew near,
Las Cruces came to mind.
A vacation in the town
they once held so dear,
but had chosen to leave behind.

"The older the crow, the weaker the breath,
the softer the heart, the sweeter the death,"
the old Indian woman cawed in their sleep,
as they flew into town from all around
to find a sense of peace.

But peace was fleeting
as All Hallow's Eve loomed
and the town prepared.
Each brought their talisman

back home to roost,
some packed it unaware.

They met at the Las Cruces Inn
on the thirty first,
each dressed in black,
and conspired to undo
the old Indian woman's curse
and leave with their souls intact.

"From beyond the grave, I'll be reborn
when the moonlight fades into the morn,"
the old Indian woman groaned
throughout the day inside the brains
of those who had been called back home.

As the Las Cruces streets
filled with kids
running from door to door,
some stopped for treats
at the Las Cruces Inn
and received something more.

Smooth round stones
with painted crows
were placed in buckets and bags.
The unsuspecting children

would go home
not knowing what they had.

And so on All Hallow's Day it came to light,
a group of elderly travelers died during the night
at the Las Cruces Inn where each of them stayed.
Each was found hands clasped, peaceful at last,
and what looked like a smile upon their face.

LILITH

Jillian A. Perkins

SHE IS A CREATURE OF THE NIGHT. MEN follow her heart rendering cries to the ends of the earth to be with her, but once; for a nights worth of desireful lust.

The pleasure is ephemeral after it turns into a blood gorging feast; the second they encounter her carnivorous nature.

From a distance she calls out to the echoing night sky, which has been waiting for her leathery wings and tainted bare skin to grace it with her presence.

Gently she whispers sweet promises into the night air, which bring her carnal stirring words to her next victim.

LILITH BY MICHAEL BIELACZYC

Autumn's Child

Kimberly Richardson

UNDER THE BLANKET OF AUTUMN
apple trees flourish,
their gift to the world presented
sweet perfume, lingering, enticing the flesh of
Nature to partake of their labor.
The leaves, regal and elderly
fall like ghost soldiers to the pine-needled
ground, self sacrificed for their own
unknown cause and reason.
This sylvan space, this green
frozen and locked in its beauty
provide many a creative one
with inspiration and free insanity.
A slow evolution, one that cannot
be taken lightly, refusing to acknowledge
the ever changing and polluting outside,
a fear that lies deep rooted and safe from
innocent eyes.
Is this place the whole of existence?
Should I be its messenger, a John the Baptist poetic

to warn the world of an imminent change,
a change to green, to flowers forever giving
their scent to overpower and kill,
of trees, golden and red, that whisper
through their branches, luring people away
under guises of comfort of Autumn?
This space, sacred, comes with longing
of souls, a desire to capture, and a feeling of lost.
And who am I who should care so
of this wood, this place of maddening beauty,
this Autumn tinged sanctuary?
I am of it, born from it,
dead because of it, living forever through it.
I am the autumn, leaves so golden and frail
scents with no definition and clean
eyes multicolored and far reaching
littered with apples, the fruit of Avalon,
my soul the result of those who dared to love
too much this place; here I sit
under the blanket of Autumn.

THE LIFE BEYOND

Rupert Brooke, 1911

HE WAKES, WHO NEVER THOUGHT TO
wake again,
Who held the end was Death. He opens eyes
Slowly, to one long livid oozing plain
Closed down by the strange eyeless heavens. He lies;
And waits; and once in timeless sick surmise
Through the dead air heaves up an unknown hand,
Like a dry branch. No life is in that land,
Himself not lives, but is a thing that cries;
An unmeaning point upon the mud; a speck
Of moveless horror; an Immortal One
Cleansed of the world, sentient and dead; a fly
Fast-stuck in grey sweat on a corpse's neck.

I thought when love for you died, I should die.
It's dead. Alone, most strangely, I live on.

The Watcher

Kimberly Richardson

HE LOOKED AT ME WITH EYES
Stolen from a creature not yet named by Man.
Such an ocular moment
Would last only seconds
And yet my body stayed rooted
To the spot, a slave and servant to what lay
Beneath the flesh, of a tease that I refused
To acknowledge.
He was here, among the glassy eyes,
Searching for someone, thing,
A possible reason for his own existence.
Never has the desire to fall on my knees
Ever been stronger – shall he think me weak
And unacceptable of this gift?
Black, like ravens, are warmer to the touches
Under my fingers; I dare not lick the
Sheen from them. His sweat shall poison me.
Within his arms are oceans, of waters
Created and destroyed every day,
Calling me like a vengeful Siren;

No sailor am I.

This, then, is the time to surrender all

And dream, lest I forget how.

PLAGUE
Dean M. Drinkel

THE POWER OF DARKNESS FORCED ME TO
My knees. Surrounded by the blue
Sea. I tried hard to breathe. But
Floating nightmares catch me.
A city in my skull, movement of
Constellations. I am a bridge with
A gun at my temple. Hold tight the
World in my arms. Embrace jeweled life.

Razors tear into my side, the
Separation of soul and flesh begins.
The butterflies take to the air.
Kissing platonic ghosts goodbye.

My life a desolate place, a cacophonic
Mystery. No hope there. Dig down
Deeper unearth a dream of sorts.
Listen to the waves, crashing into the city.

THE LONELY MAN

Jeffrey Barnes

THE LONELY MAN CLOSED HIS EYES
He heard the hiss of water against sand
The occasional crash of a curling wave

The lonely man felt within for peace

The lonely man eyes still closed
Felt heat as of the sun
Shining down on a calm clear day

The lonely man found his peace

The lonely man opened his eyes
He heard the hiss of rot at the window
The occasional crash of body on building

The lonely man felt within for acceptance

The lonely man eyes still open
Felt heat from the storefront heater
Shining in defiance of the end of man

The lonely man found his acceptance

The lonely man waited in sadness
Without fear
Waited for the sound of breaking glass
And the rush of cold air.

EGO TE ABSOLVO

Dean M. Drinkel

I SAW THE CITY WEEPING.
The pain was hard to resist.
Hid in tempered dreams but
Still I drank the bitter liquid
That led us to this insanity.

The girl pulled the dagger from the
Chamberlain's heart. Her obsession
Was satiated, she knew that
She was not the only one.
But the taste of his salty flesh
Calmed her, if only temporarily.

"Kill for me." The army of charred
Buzzards cried. The child tore
From his face the metallic mask,
Revealing the putrid flesh of the world
Beneath. The anger behind the fear.
Dead souls took flight: destination unknown.

A QUIET CORNER
Richard Evans

WHEN MY TIME IS DONE
lay me down in a quiet corner,
an acorn and steel in my hands
and I shall watch over others forevermore.

Strong I shall grow
and in my shade shelter those that come
to see those that have gone before
to keep the promise of freedom.

Lay me down in a quiet corner
next to my friends who took up arms,
Guardian Wolves amongst the sheep;
Keepers of the ways to our freedom.

No longer shall I spill the blood
that called me to those far off fields
but shades I shall lay in this
quiet corner of mine.
Others shall rise anew,
sing the anthems of freedom.

The spirits inside cry for it
and shall not be denied;
but for fear they let others march ahead
and take up cold iron
and forge a bond beyond counting
with those who would march at their side.

From my quiet corner I shall sleep
and pray I'm called never again.
But bury me with a seed and a promise
I shall nurture the roots of the trees.
In the shade you can rest and sleep
safe for the one who stood.

Tis a choice, my friend, in the end;
to walk far afield, steel in hand
In far off lands for the cries of freedom;
to earn scars and still smile as your friends fall to the
　　side
to never rise again.

Bury them too, with seed and steel in hand.

And in our quiet corner,
a wooded glade of peace,
we shall wait, faithful always,
for when the call comes once again.

For as we grow so shall the children;
and amongst them the wolves still roam
who hear the call of the winds of freedom
through the trees of our quiet corner.

SWEET SORROW BY BOB GIADROSICH

CHAPTER 3:

SWEET SORROW

PARTING IS SUCH SWEET SORROW—WHAT a contemptible lie!

And when that parting rents the veil of night and invites the darkness in, the emotional pain may be sharp, but never so severe as that first night alone, when the one for which you care is forever out of reach, whether real or imagined.

And no one, but another, can shield you, and hold back the night.

ANNABEL LEE

Edgar Allan Poe, 1849

IT WAS MANY AND MANY A YEAR AGO,
In a kingdom by the sea,
That a maiden lived whom you may know
By the name of Annabel Lee;—
And this maiden she lived with no other thought
Than to love and be loved by me.

I was a child and She was a child,
In this kingdom by the sea,
But we loved with a love that was more than love—
I and my Annabel Lee—
With a love that the wingéd seraphs of Heaven
Coveted her and me.

And this was the reason that, long ago,
In this kingdom by the sea,
A wind blew out of a cloud by night
Chilling my Annabel Lee;
So that her high-born kinsmen came
And bore her away from me,

To shut her up, in a sepulchre
In this kingdom by the sea.

The angels, not half so happy in Heaven,
Went envying her and me;
Yes! that was the reason (as all men know,
In this kingdom by the sea)
That the wind came out of the cloud, chilling
And killing my Annabel Lee.

But our love it was stronger by far than the love
Of those who were older than we—
Of many far wiser than we—
And neither the angels in Heaven above
Nor the demons down under the sea
Can ever dissever my soul from the soul
Of the beautiful Annabel Lee:—

For the moon never beams without bringing me dreams
Of the beautiful Annabel Lee;
And the stars never rise but I see the bright eyes
Of the beautiful Annabel Lee;
And so, all the night-tide, I lie down by the side
Of my darling, my darling, my life and my bride
In her sepulchre there by the sea—
In her tomb by the side of the sea.

AND THOU ART DEAD, AS YOUNG AND FAIR

George Gordon (Lord) Byron, 1812

AND THOU ART DEAD, AS YOUNG AND
fair
As aught of mortal birth;
And form so soft, and charms so rare,
Too soon return'd to Earth!
Though Earth receiv'd them in her bed,
And o'er the spot the crowd may tread
In carelessness or mirth,
There is an eye which could not brook
A moment on that grave to look.

I will not ask where thou liest low,
Nor gaze upon the spot;
There flowers or weeds at will may grow,
So I behold them not:
It is enough for me to prove
That what I lov'd, and long must love,
Like common earth can rot;
To me there needs no stone to tell,
'T is Nothing that I lov'd so well.

Yet did I love thee to the last

As fervently as thou,

Who didst not change through all the past,

And canst not alter now.

The love where Death has set his seal,

Nor age can chill, nor rival steal,

Nor falsehood disavow:

And, what were worse, thou canst not see

Or wrong, or change, or fault in me.

The better days of life were ours;

The worst can be but mine:

The sun that cheers, the storm that lowers,

Shall never more be thine.

The silence of that dreamless sleep

I envy now too much to weep;

Nor need I to repine

That all those charms have pass'd away,

I might have watch'd through long decay.

The flower in ripen'd bloom unmatch'd

Must fall the earliest prey;

Though by no hand untimely snatch'd,

The leaves must drop away:

And yet it were a greater grief

To watch it withering, leaf by leaf,

Than see it pluck'd to-day;

Since earthly eye but ill can bear

To trace the change to foul from fair.

I know not if I could have borne
To see thy beauties fade;
The night that follow'd such a morn
Had worn a deeper shade:
Thy day without a cloud hath pass'd,
And thou wert lovely to the last,
Extinguish'd, not decay'd;
As stars that shoot along the sky
Shine brightest as they fall from high.

As once I wept, if I could weep,
My tears might well be shed,
To think I was not near to keep
One vigil o'er thy bed;
To gaze, how fondly! on thy face,
To fold thee in a faint embrace,
Uphold thy drooping head;
And show that love, however vain,
Nor thou nor I can feel again.

Yet how much less it were to gain,
Though thou hast left me free,
The loveliest things that still remain,
Than thus remember thee!
The all of thine that cannot die
Through dark and dread Eternity
Returns again to me,
And more thy buried love endears
Than aught except its living years.

LOVE AND DEATH

George Gordon (Lord) Byron, 1887

I WATCHED THEE WHEN THE FOE WAS AT OUR
side,
Ready to strike at him —- or thee and me,
Were safety hopeless —- rather than divide
Aught with one loved save love and liberty.
I watched thee on the breakers, when the rock,
Received our prow, and all was storm and fear,
And bade thee cling to me through every shock;
This arm would be thy bark, or breast thy bier.
I watched thee when the fever glazed thine eyes,
Yielding my couch and stretched me on the ground
When overworn with watching, ne'er to rise
From thence if thou an early grave hadst found.
The earthquake came, and rocked the quivering wall,
And men and nature reeled as if with wine.
Whom did I seek around the tottering hall?
For thee. Whose safety first provide for? Thine.
And when convulsive throes denied my breath
The faintest utterance to my fading thought,
To thee —- to thee —- e'en in the gasp of death

My spirit turned, oh ! oftener than it ought.

Thus much and more, and yet thou lov'st me not,

And never wilt ! Love dwells not in our will.

Nor can I blame thee, though it be my lot

To strongly, wrongly, vainly love thee still.

"Out, Out–"

Robert Frost, 1916

THE BUZZ-SAW SNARLED AND RATTLED IN the yard
And made dust and dropped stove-length sticks of wood,

Sweet-scented stuff when the breeze drew across it.

And from there those that lifted eyes could count

Five mountain ranges one behind the other

Under the sunset far into Vermont.

And the saw snarled and rattled, snarled and rattled,

As it ran light, or had to bear a load.

And nothing happened: day was all but done.

Call it a day, I wish they might have said

To please the boy by giving him the half hour

That a boy counts so much when saved from work.

His sister stood beside them in her apron
To tell them "Supper." At the word, the saw,
As if to prove saws knew what supper meant,
Leaped out at the boy's hand, or seemed to leap—
He must have given the hand. However it was,
Neither refused the meeting. But the hand!
The boy's first outcry was a rueful laugh,
As he swung toward them holding up the hand
Half in appeal, but half as if to keep
The life from spilling. Then the boy saw all—
Since he was old enough to know, big boy
Doing a man's work, though a child at heart—
He saw all spoiled. "Don't let him cut my hand off—
The doctor, when he comes. Don't let him, sister!"
So. But the hand was gone already.
The doctor put him in the dark of ether.
He lay and puffed his lips out with his breath.
And then—the watcher at his pulse took fright.
No one believed. They listened at his heart.
Little—less—nothing!—and that ended it.
No more to build on there. And they, since they
Were not the one dead, turned to their affairs.

The Pang More Sharp Than All

An Allegory

Samuel Taylor Coleridge, 1825

I

HE TOO HAS FLITTED FROM HIS SECRET
nest,
Hope's last and dearest child without a
name!—
Has flitted from me, like the warmthless flame,
That makes false promise of a place of rest
To the tired Pilgrim's still believing mind;
Or like some Elfin Knight in kingly court,
Who having won all guerdons in his sport,
Glides out of view, and whither none can find!

II

YES! HE HATH FLITTED FROM ME—WITH
what aim,
Or why, I know not! 'Twas a home of bliss,

And he was innocent, as the pretty shame
Of babe, that tempts and shuns the menaced kiss,
From its twy-cluster'd hiding place of snow!
Pure as the babe, I ween, and all aglow
As the dear hopes, that swell the mother's breast—
Her eyes down gazing o'er her claspéd charge;—
Yet gay as that twice happy father's kiss,
That well might glance aside, yet never miss,
Where the sweet mark emboss'd so sweet a targe—
Twice wretched he who hath been doubly blest!

III

LIKE A LOOSE BLOSSOM ON A GUSTY
night
He flitted from me—and has left behind
(As if to them his faith he ne'er did plight)
Of either sex and answerable mind
Two playmates, twin-births of his foster-dame:
The one a steady lad (Esteem he hight)
And Kindness is the gentler sister's name.
Dim likeness now, though fair she be and good,
Of that bright Boy who hath us all forsook;
But in his full-eyed aspect when she stood,
And while her face reflected every look,
And in reflection kindled—she became
So like Him, that almost she seem'd the same!

IV

AH! HE IS GONE, AND YET WILL NOT
depart!—
Is with me still, yet I from him exiled!
For still there lives within my secret heart
The magic image of the magic Child,
Which there he made up-grow by his strong art,
As in that crystal orb—wise Merlin's feat,—
The wondrous 'World of Glass,' wherein inisled
All long'd-for things their beings did repeat;—
And there he left it, like a Sylph beguiled,
To live and yearn and languish incomplete!

V

CAN WIT OF MAN A HEAVIER GRIEF
reveal?
Can sharper pang from hate or scorn arise?
Yes! one more sharp there is that deeper lies,
Which fond Esteem but mocks when he would heal.
Yet neither scorn nor hate did it devise,
But sad compassion and atoning zeal!
One pang more blighting-keen than hope betray'd!
And this it is my woeful hap to feel,
When, at her Brother's hest, the twin-born Maid
With face averted and unsteady eyes,

Her truant playmate's faded robe puts on;
And inly shrinking from her own disguise
Enacts the faery Boy that's lost and gone.
O worse than all! O pang all pangs above
Is Kindness counterfeiting absent Love!

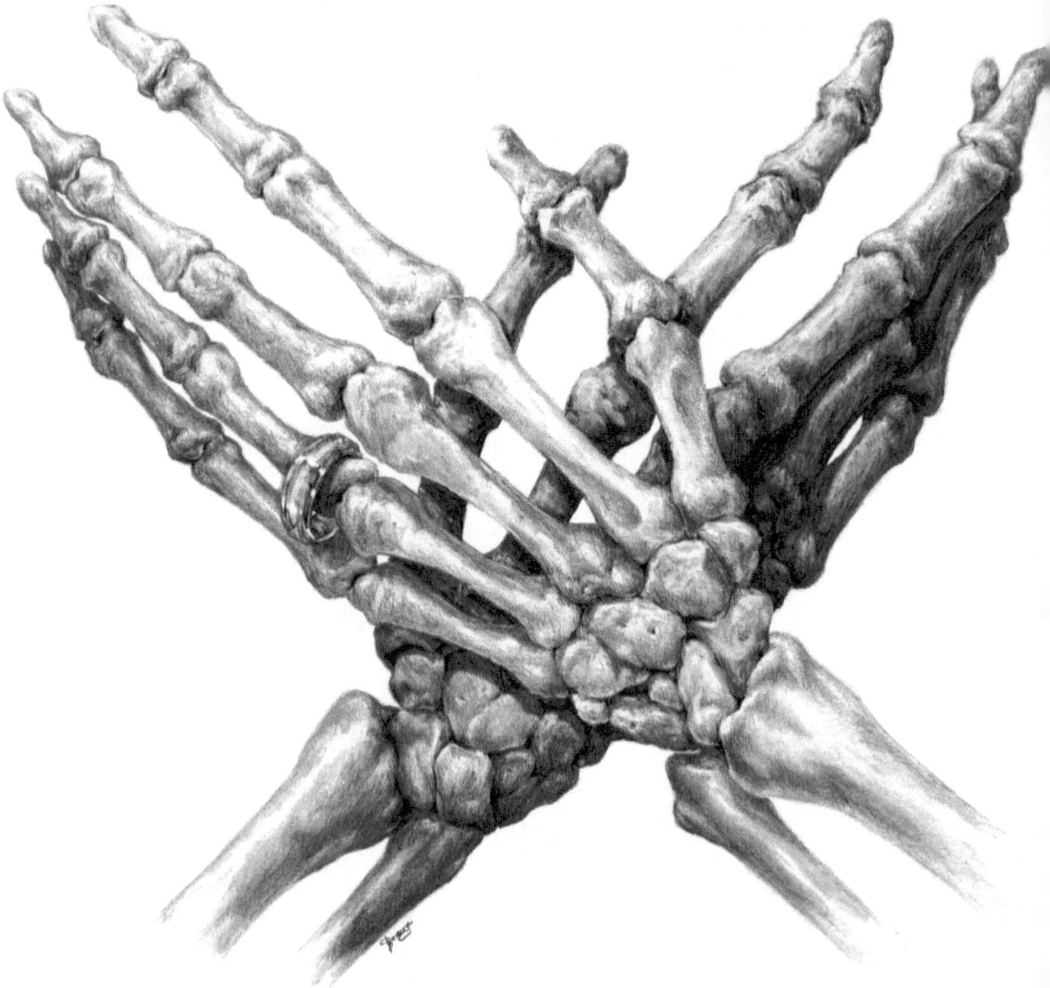

'TIL DEATH BY PAUL BIELACZYC

VICE VERSA

Ambrose Bierce, 1903

OWN IN THE STATE OF MAINE, THE story goes,
A woman, to secure a lapsing pension,
Married a soldier—though the good Lord knows
That very common act scarce calls for mention.
What makes it worthy to be writ and read—
The man she married had been nine hours dead!
Now, marrying a corpse is not an act
Familiar to our daily observation,
And so I crave her pardon if the fact
Suggests this interesting speculation:
Should some mischance restore the man to life
Would she be then a widow, or a wife?
Let casuists contest the point; I'm not
Disposed to grapple with so great a matter.
'T would tie my thinker in a double knot
And drive me staring mad as any hatter—
Though I submit that hatters are, in fact,
Sane, and all other human beings cracked.

Small thought have I of Destiny or Chance;
Luck seems to me the same thing as Intention;
In metaphysics I could ne'er advance,
And think it of the Devil's own invention.
Enough of joy to know though when I wed

I must be married, yet I may be dead.

BELOVED WARRIOR

Janet and Chris Morris

WHAT DID THEY DO THAT I CANNOT do,

your bold-tongued leaders who enflamed your fierce desire?

Now you are hot for fighting.

You long to throw yourself against the body of your
enemy, not mine;

and pierce his flesh, not mine.

What did they say, your bold-tongued leaders,

that I cannot say to win your love?

How now shall I pray, when you have battle
pounding in your blood

and your heart is hard like bronze?

Come back to me unbroken, unharmed.

You live to breathe war's fury.

I live for the sight of you returning,

your fine skin covered in armor, your beautiful head
covered in glory,

your bright shield and your ash spear in your hand.

Come back to me.

Paintbrush and Paracelsus

Michael H. Hanson

AS INJURED SOUL FESTERS, BLEEDS,
softly weeps,
my eyes reach out for comfort and surcease —
in abject appeal to ancient healers.

With salves of talc, white spirit, and resin
I'm wrapped inside stretched canvas bandages
as safflow'r, walnut, and poppy seed oils
cleanse and purify aching psychic wounds.

Silent watchers, doorways into beauty,
framed across bland and tan apartment walls —
idyllic visions and soothing colors
allay... sanctify my humanity.

DROWNING SORROWS ISN'T ENOUGH, YOU HAVE TO CHOKE THEM

Louis Agresta

LAST NIGHT, I PLOTTED YOUR DEATH

Imagine that!

I sat down and put my mind to killing you

Amazing

Picture it

While you were home (maybe alone),

reading a book

or maybe just resting

your head with

that little tilt

you have just so

I sat beside my phone

And figured out a way to kill you

I didn't plan it alone

Now don't worry, its no one you know

Just an old friend, I knew I could count on

In fact,

There are a number of people in on this
and I'm planning on adding more
— years and years of more —
(if that's what it takes)
and one day there may even be so many
that my phone book will shrivel up and turn black
In fact,
I think I'll fill up a book with names of people
who'll help me murder you
Your murder
Imagine that!

So there I was
just off the phone
picturing you alone in bed, dozing, while the radio
    droned
(Actually, I must confess I know you weren't alone)
and feeling rather satisfied
that I'd figured out a fool proof means of ending you
Then I went out for a pack of cigarettes
(my brand, not yours)
all very calm and very cool
and you hadn't even a clue
Incredible
Of course not a single clue

Outside
the wind slipped
cold and lonely as a mirror
lost stumbling on silent streets
it echoed like the cries of forgotten times
through sepulcher hearts
the wind swept
the wind wept, and in one sharp moment
and the ice clear night bit with the teeth of self
    conscience
and tore the flesh from my satisfaction
and told me just how lonely it will be when the dead
    are lost
lonely as a tomb
lonely as a wake
lonely as my bed

And the Moon rolled over buildings and familiar
    streets
crushing them like sand, a rolling weight of lunar
    memories
and I ran, stumbled, ran again
the night followed, rumbling, at my heels
smashed aside the mausoleum doors
caught me, pushed me against the concrete walls
and raped me with its whisper
with its secret

its wisdom
and left me to weep
with not even the wind for company

Imagine that!

I'll still going to kill you, you know
Nothing can save me from it, drown you
In fact,
the night taught me nothing
not really
it just passed on a reminder
when you die
I die
and we'll have a funeral only one will attend
and I will bury us together
in my sepulcher heart

Imagine that

CALLIOPE

Michael H. Hanson

O H HORROR OF ALL HORRORS KNOWN
and spiteful dark unholy deeds
the ghastly shriek and fading moan
the death of my Calliope.

This nightmare born of wicked dream
this tortured tale of murdered wife
assassins claimed her while asleep
and killed my love with poisoned knife.

And so I found her 'pon our bed
and so I prayed this mortal plea
to trade my life for her instead
I begged the Lord to intervene.

That brutish spirit caring not
immune to tears and prostrating
that God of Abraham and Lot
ignored all of my suffering.

Damn all of Heaven's offerings

damn all the learned holy priests
and damn their cold baptismal springs
and promise of eternity!

Calliope! Calliope!
I birth an awful hopeless scream
and pledge this dark unwholesome oath
to take revenge on Heaven's liege.

And so I claim the midnight throne
and all evils crawling beneath
and so I prey on Yahweh's hosts
and on their innocence I feast.

LAMENT FOR THE CHILDREN OF ELENDIL

Richard Groller

THEY CAME AS DESTROYERS
our rivals of old
to the place where we lived
and we loved and grew old
where we raised all our children
and tended our fields
in peace there was justice
without it we reeled
from the senseless marauding,
the blood and the slaughter
unleashed on the gentle sweet people
the children of Elendil.

For this is death
eternal death
in silence forever
the icy cold fingers
and the narrowing light
and the bodies they left to the darkness

as the life force escapes
until all you have left is the terror of night
and the darkness of space
and the lingering echo that hangs in the air
of the mothers that cried
with their last dying breath "Not the children!"

Their emissaries came,
bearing branches of olive
'twas peace that they sought
their desired objective
turn your swords into plowshares
and we'll do the same
we will all live as brothers
and justice will reign
and the sweet trusting people desirous of peace
believed their entreaties and held a great feast,
destroyed all their weapons and let up a cheer
for their hopes and their dreams of the future were
    here
And Death was the fate of the trusting,
the children of Elendil.

For this is death
eternal death
in silence forever

the icy cold fingers
and the narrowing light
and the bodies they left to the darkness
as the life force escapes
until all you have left is the terror of night
and the darkness of space
and the lingering echo that hangs in the air
of the mothers that cried
with their last dying breath "Not the children!"

No lament nor a cry
for a world that is gone
not a tale to be told
nor a song to be sung
for the people that lived
and the people that died
for not one of them's left
not even one child...
only far distant echoes
and sleep shattered dreams
in the minds of the butchers
who wake up with screams on
remembering the faces of those
they had seen
at their moment of death
but especially those of the children.

For this is death
eternal death
in silence forever
the icy cold fingers
and the narrowing light
and the bodies they left to the darkness
as the life force escapes
until all you have left is the terror of night
and the darkness of space
and the pain and the sorrow again and again
as they whispered in vain
with their last ounce of strength "Not the children!"

SORROW SONG

Louis Agresta

WHEN LOVE WAS LOST, LOST WAS
love…
the sun no longer shines, but settles like a
greasy film
on the skin of reality
making buildings improbable and out of place
while the church steeple, with its pigeon house eyes,
from the bitterness of aging,
frowns green envy on its town
of emptied streets and trash

candy wrappers, fleeing echoes
flit like spurts of laughter or children's dreams
in the wind, tattered and tempting

i grab for one, and fall into the street
where the curbs, like Alice walls, grow large
and the wind isn't wind
it is cold

when love was lost, lost was love…

i leave you, muffled in a gauzy moment,
stumble into an impossible alleyway of desire:
curbed and dirty and paved
where fat people stare into bakery windows,
stores whose names i'll never know,
empty cars go nowhere,
parked cars seek streetlight comfort,
and give ambush rights
to every passing beggar, begging me to give what's
    gone
where couples, gripping hands, cleave
as if to fire in a wasted Klondike town, seek warmth,
find only melt on sour skin, on clothes
i fled below,
i fled within

when love was lost, lost was love…

i remember when I first passed these darkened gates
shiny turnstiles, ground me through like meaty gears,
to happiness or tears
i knew not which

and in the Belly,
City women brokered loneliness
down passageways to work and sin
in wail, in steel and screech

i fled again
and passed again within

to the subway, our wedding car
rumbling mindless through corridors of wasted time
the hall is nearly empty now, the few remaining
    guests
locked in willed separation across a dirty aisle
never touching

in vain i seek to stand,
keep place and pace
amid slim metallic milestones of silver memory,
which cut the path into a mockery
and an obstacle course

once i could walk our church from front to fore
balanced, in the shifting car, but
in the end, i am left with a sliding door to exit
and a map like a butterfly under glass

when love was lost, lost was love…

and in the Belly,
City men purchase loneliness
down hallways lined with Wall Street clout
by screech, by wail and rumble

i fled again
and passed again without

through two-way meat-grinder spindle teeth
as the wind hurled down the concrete mouth
around the throat-bound prison booth,
whirled, whistled, whispered,
ancient north spirit and enemy,
ancient songs of mockery,
it laughed as choice-less, i emerged
and we embraced

the barren concrete paths and broken men
in their bitter ends,
left with only strength to beg the wind,
do not leave me, only friend…

when love was lost, lost was love…

i strolled with strangers through beggar's bedrooms
poured over cheap art for hours in cheaper stores,
it was all
the distance in a telescope upended
music an illusion,
dead trees hung between deader hands,
for the fruitless hope of Calgary
it was all

dripping needles and drying sap
and too, too many children pushed and pulled
and carted about by blue-lipped servants
the only pleasant sight, the dogs,
whose claws click-clacked on foreign concrete
    wrongly,
and panted in the wind, noses chewing happily on
    fleeting odors
while tired towers of complex stone
struggled to ignore it all

hunger and a diner pulled me in…

they fed me food like wood paste gruel
cruelly forced from a stubborn tube
disgorged upon my plate by lovers of false advertising
promising nourishment and satisfaction

amid the babble of a hundred faceless, feasting
    patrons,
i watched the toungeless masses mouth their meals
    without complaint
while i with concrete lips, chewed my windy paste in
    silence
and all our eating noises blurred into one vast,
    incomprehensible language

Ah Misery! She Maketh Me to Lie Down on Diner
    Tiles
Bathe in Neon and Crouch on Late Night Stairs

when i found you again,

you were gone,

the gauzy moment blown to absence

by the din of passing earthquakes

and our pointless, petty private wars

Now who shall hear my Sorrow Song?

none.

none, but I,

and I alone shall mourn

when Love was lost, lost was love.

A TASTE OF THE BITTER

Jack William Finley

ICE COLD FINGERS WRAP 'ROUND A RAZOR
sharp blade of lies and betrayal
My heart lies rotting at the bottom of a bloody sea
of treachery and deceit
The blade still twisting
Delicate fingers trace back to the villain I once called
friend
Words of blood from the great and powerful Book of
Infinite Woe
Greater love hath no man than that he would give up
his life for his friends
So much more the sorrow to turn to those you
thought were friends and find only the shadow of
ghosts whispering their poisonous deceits on the
sharp cold winds of endless night.
What greater sin? What fool hardy endeavor to trust
your soul to the hands of vile creatures who thrust
the knife from the blackest pits of Hell
My fortress is built of sorrow and loneliness
My shield is forged of purest despair

I sink to darkest depths like ancient and forgotten
  gods and forge my sword and spear of the purest
  hate.
I will rise again forged anew in the fires of damnation
  and seek vengeance on those I foolishly once
  called friend

Limbo-God Only Knows

Richard Groller

A RESTLESS NIGHT;
a point of light; one called by the infinite;
death, then darkness, befalls the wanderer.

I dreamt my dad,
was lying on a mortuary slab.
I awoke and wept.
It was true.

As they closed the coffin
I kissed him good bye with a tear from my eye

that I pressed to his lips.
My hand held his a final time,
and in our palms was cupped another tear
as I bid him painful adieu.....

He wanders.
I wonder if.
We are in Limbo
celestial, terrestrial, it's all the same,
except he was; I am.

Hand in hand,
in the recesses of my mind,
we search the mists of time together
for heaven, hell or purgatory.
Yet, we are strangers still,
never knowing each other,
then or now.

All alone and deep in my soul,
I walked the night with him.
We found only Limbo, then parted.
God only knows why we are.
God only knows, will we ever meet again.

The Soul That Knew No Solace

Kurt Newton

THOSE CURSED CHAINS OF GRIEF THAT
bound me,
   That kept me prisoner of unspeakable things
I wished had never found me,
But I devised a way to escape those painful memories
that circled around me:
I gave up my very soul.

And once my soul was forever forsaken,
My nightly excesses became uncontrolled,
now served by a conscience that would never
   awaken.
It's cold, I know, but I traveled the road
many have dreamed but few have taken;
But, for this, there was a price.

And the price was for every unholy behavior,
A piece of my body would wither and die,
revealing the depths of my true nature,

A finger, an ear, a patch of hair, an eye—
in the mirror I became a hideous stranger;
I didn't know how but it had to stop.

So I searched for the soul I had so callously
    abandoned;
I found it in the eyes and smile of my three-year old
    niece
in whom innocence still lay pure and undamaged.
I prayed that the Gods would accept the sacrifice of
    one so sweet
in return for the one thing I demanded,
And returned my soul they did.

Now here I am whole again,
But these chains of grief still bind me
down deep in my soul again,
And keep me prisoner of unspeakable things,
irredeemable things that are sure to take their toll
    again.
Her face will haunt me to my grave.

To The Rising Full Moon

Johann Wolfgang von Goethe, 1828

Translation by Edgar A. Bowring, 1853

WILT THOU SUDDENLY ENSHROUD
thee,
Who this moment wert so nigh?
Heavy rising masses cloud thee,
Thou art hidden from mine eye.
Yet my sadness thou well knowest,
Gleaming sweetly as a star!
That I'm loved, 'tis thou that showest,
Though my loved one may be far.
Upward mount then! clearer, milder,
Robed in splendour far more bright!
Though my heart with grief throbs wilder,
Fraught with rapture is the night!

PUMPKIN IN THE SKY BY LIZ HOLLAND

THE COTTAGE ON THE LAKE

Kurt Newton

THE RENTAL AGENT SMILED AS I SIGNED
my name on the winter lease,
along with a check for security deposit plus
first and last month's rent.
She nervously shook my hand and promptly handed
me the keys,
"Good luck," she said, then hurried out the door, got
into her car and left.

I didn't understand how a lakeside cottage so
beautiful could be so cheap,
fully furnished, kitchen appliances, utilities included
in the monthly check.
I moved my belongings in that weekend and on the
first night, before I went to sleep,
I spent the last hour of the evening in a chair alone
upon the deck.

The night air blew fresh and warm across the surface
    of the lake,
the lap of the water, the creak of the dock, such
    peaceful sounds to my ear.
But when I heard the whisper I at first believed it was
    a neighbor staying up late,
but the adjacent cottages were dark and unoccupied
    this time of year.

I thought nothing of it and went to bed, exhausted
    from the move,
but that night I dreamed of a woman in a sleeping
    gown standing on the dock,
staring out across the open water under the light of a
    pregnant moon.
I rushed to prevent her from jumping in, but before I
    could I heard the clock.

My morning alarm woke me up to another brilliant
    autumn day,
another pleasant realization that was just too hard to
    believe.
I was once again on my own and in a beautiful
    cottage on the lake,
where I could spend my hours alone with no
    pressures placed on me.

But when nighttime fell and surrounded the cottage
with its dark,
I found myself looking out the window for reasons I
could not explain.
Once again, before going to bed, I sat outside beneath
the stars,
and watched the moonlight slither like a serpent
across the lake.

This time I was awakened from my resting spot atop
the deck,
by the sobbing of a young woman who stood on the
wooden dock below.
I got up and slowly approached her, the breeze a soft
caress.
"Hello?" I said. She turned and, though startled, made
no move to go.

She had long dark hair and eyes as sad as flowers in
the rain,
and she wore only a sleeping gown with no shoes
upon her feet.
I invited her to leave the water and come inside my
cottage on the lake,
but she smiled the saddest smile and then threw
herself into the deep.

I woke up then, my hands still gripping tight the deck
    chair arms,
my heart pounding like a hammer nailing spikes into
    my chest.
She was gone, this woman, this apparition, this love
    reflection, she was gone,
and I was never, ever going to get her back again.

The days and months that followed were a silent
    wintery chill,
spent in the company of myself both in dream and
    wide awake.
I have to say I loved the one who came to visit and
    always will,
the one who lies beneath the water at the cottage on
    the lake.

The Dark Seduction

Allan Gilbreath

THE SUN RULES THE DAY.
The moon rules the night.
No matter what your pain is
I will set things right.

Are you lonely in your life?
Has your heart been betrayed?
Give your love to me
and those feelings will fade.

Are you always struggling?
Are you misunderstood?
I will always listen to you.
I will always treat you good.

Are things too complicated?
Are the decisions too tough?
Let me handle all the choices,
You've already had enough.

Does your family bother you.
They just won't let you be.

You don't need to talk to them.
All you need now is me.

I will solve all your problems.
I will be your shining knight.
Just do as only I say
and everything will be all right.

Don't worry about your old friends,
just put all your faith in me.
I will give you new friends.
You will like them, you'll see.

It is my pleasure to help.
I ask so little in return,
just your complete obedience.
It's not that hard to learn.

Your old life is completely gone.
Everything is brand new.
I have shut out the world.
I have done it all for you.

Finally, where your hopes do shine,
I will put out that light
because now you live in the darkness
of my eternal night.

THE MOON OF OTHER DAYS

Rudyard Kipling, 1915

BENEATH THE DEEP VERANDA'S SHADE,
When bats begin to fly,
I sit me down and watch—alas!—
Another evening die.
Blood-red behind the sere ferash
She rises through the haze.
Sainted Diana! can that be
The Moon of Other Days?
Ah! shade of little Kitty Smith,
Sweet Saint of Kensington!
Say, was it ever thus at Home
The Moon of August shone,
When arm in arm we wandered long
Through Putney's evening haze,
And Hammersmith was Heaven beneath
The Moon of Other Days?
But Wandle's stream is Sutlej now,
And Putney's evening haze

The dust that half a hundred kine

Before my window raise.

Unkempt, unclean, athwart the mist

The seething city looms,

In place of Putney's golden gorse

The sickly babul blooms.

Glare down, old Hecate, through the dust,

And bid the pie-dog yell,

Draw from the drain its typhoid-germ,

From each bazaar its smell;

Yea, suck the fever from the tank

And sap my strength therewith:

Thank Heaven, you show a smiling face

To little Kitty Smith!

THE VISION OF THE ARCHANGELS

Rupert Brooke, 1915

SLOWLY UP SILENT PEAKS, THE WHITE EDGE of the world,
Trod four archangels, clear against the unheeding
    sky,
Bearing, with quiet even steps, and great wings furled,
A little dingy coffin; where a child must lie,
It was so tiny. (Yet, you had fancied, God could never
Have bidden a child turn from the spring and the
    sunlight,
And shut him in that lonely shell, to drop for ever
Into the emptiness and silence, into the night. . . .)

They then from the sheer summit cast, and watched
    it fall,
Through unknown glooms, that frail black coffin —
    and therein
God's little pitiful Body lying, worn and thin,
And curled up like some crumpled, lonely flower-
    petal —

SWEET SORROW

Till it was no more visible; then turned again
With sorrowful quiet faces downward to the plain.

REQUIESCAT

Oscar Wilde, 1881

TREAD LIGHTLY, SHE IS NEAR
Under the snow,
Speak gently, she can hear
The daisies grow.
All her bright golden hair
Tarnished with rust,
She that was young and fair
Fallen to dust.
Lily-like, white as snow,
She hardly knew
She was a woman, so
Sweetly she grew.
Coffin-board, heavy stone,
Lie on her breast;
I vex my heart alone,
She is at rest.

Peace, peace; she cannot hear
Lyre or sonnet;
All my life's buried here,
Heap earth upon it.

I Am Here

Kimberly Richardson

HELP ME.
I have forgotten where I have been
for it is too late to reclaim.
Standing, I fall to the floor
unaware that I am already dead.
My hair, dry and tasteless
taken from me, a denial of life.
Give me water, but that would not be enough
to cover the scabs I received as a child.
Not enough.
Fortunately, I am still here
alone, too strong to walk away,
a shade too forceful and lacking grace.
Denial of pleasures, making me less than Roman
my arms frail and reaching, always reaching.
Forgive the insults I have created of myself
when my coughs bring up precious blood
and tears–this is truly a sign.
For when the metallic taste is gone
and my tears are made into tea

I shall burn them all-
a virgin, sacrificing herself
complete and unashamed, a liberty
that began so long ago.
I want to be dead.
Dead, as in not living, you do understand?
Dead, as in, he left me again
to pursue fantasies
and cream coloured women singing in French.
I forgot to wave goodbye
when he sailed to that distant shore
to find himself.
I envy him for the spark he stole from me
because he is going to use it
rather than keep it dusty.
But, I am here.

THE ENTOMBMENT

Dean M. Drinkel

NOT YET DEAD, BUT THE SHADOWS approach.

Grief commences. Though the tears fall,
Eyes are dry. This is the weeping time.
Like a tide, the ebb and flow of life.
Christ, my head hurts. Is this how it was for you?
When did all this begin? Darkness in a world of
    colour.
Sepia photographs still between moving images,
Silence where sound should reign supreme. Blackened
Notes, the devil's chord. God's umbilical lost.

You are unmoving, breathing for all humanity.
Pain etched into your skin, the flesh transparent, but
    bright.
Bones withered and bent, cavorting amongst the
    carrion.
Such devotion from the damned.

There you are, hovering between this world and the
    next.

Signs of life, like a child: nursed and cared for.
Tongue tied, your lips betray me. But does it matter?
We are all where we are. An echo in someone else's
   dream.
I should have kissed you.

THE DEAD

Kimberly Richardson

THE DEAD ARE NEVER LOVED.
Strange, then, that they
Live in the minds of
The sybaritic and adulterous.
Cold blue lips touching a dried brow
Is an experience so soon over.
Hands tremble while eyes forecast
The upcoming storm, filling the
Skies with unchained howls.
Their bones, powdering rot, are
Not a comfort as to why we are here.
We are here, correct?
No, never could it ever be that simple.
The dead never listen
To pleas unfettered after the rain.

ADORATION-DESOLATION

Dean M. Drinkel

BLACK CLOUDS, ZODIAC FORTRESSES IN
the sky.
Ocean drowned corpses, scarlet ribbons criss-
cross
The flesh. Concrete creatures now reign supreme.
Explosions deep within the marrow, souls bereft of
Faith.

The twisted metal hell beckons. Did the Earth move
For you too? I should have said how I felt...but as
The sycophants of Abaddon disembark iron ships, we
all
Dance in frenzied adoration. Our mouths clamp shut
Famished nonetheless.

A storm ensues. Wooden castles bend and buckle
In the tempest. The doors to the slaughterhouse blow
open.
Decapitation, decimation, desolation rules. Where are
The beautiful people? Like us, drunk on blood, fed on

Charred flesh, monsters all. Hatred within.

The River of Despair winds through the body politic.
We shouldn't have ignored our hearts, the electronic
    pulses.
Anarchist or Antichrist, the blind vote nonetheless.
Now none fear the sky will fall. Fixated instead with
    the
Abyss, dig their own path to destruction.

Shall we share the fork?

THE ERL-KING

Johann Wolfgang von Goethe, 1782

Translation by Edgar A. Bowring, 1853

WHO RIDES THERE SO LATE THROUGH the night dark and drear?
The father it is, with his infant so dear;
He holdeth the boy tightly clasp'd in his arm,
He holdeth him safely, he keepeth him warm.

"My son, wherefore seek'st thou thy face thus to
    hide?"
"Look, father, the Erl-King is close by our side!
Dost see not the Erl-King, with crown and with
    train?"
"My son, 'tis the mist rising over the plain."

"Oh, come, thou dear infant! oh come thou with me!
Full many a game I will play there with thee;
On my strand, lovely flowers their blossoms unfold,
My mother shall grace thee with garments of gold."

"My father, my father, and dost thou not hear
The words that the Erl-King now breathes in mine
    ear?"
"Be calm, dearest child, 'tis thy fancy deceives;

'Tis the sad wind that sighs through the withering
    leaves."
"Wilt go, then, dear infant, wilt go with me there?
My daughters shall tend thee with sisterly care
My daughters by night their glad festival keep,
They'll dance thee, and rock thee, and sing thee to
    sleep."
"My father, my father, and dost thou not see,
How the Erl-King his daughters has brought here for
    me?"
"My darling, my darling, I see it aright,
'Tis the aged grey willows deceiving thy sight."
"I love thee, I'm charm'd by thy beauty, dear boy!
And if thou'rt unwilling, then force I'll employ."
"My father, my father, he seizes me fast,
Full sorely the Erl-King has hurt me at last."
The father now gallops, with terror half wild,
He grasps in his arms the poor shuddering child;
He reaches his courtyard with toil and with dread,—
The child in his arms finds he motionless, dead.

DYING INSIDE BY BOB GIADROSICH

CHAPTER 4:

THROUGH A GLASS DARKLY

TAKE A LITTLE STROLL ON THE DARK side and see what denizens lurk beyond. City streets and forest glens are equally at risk where the wild things roam. You will find the worst fiends are the ones conjured by the mind and heart, where the dark urges we all contain, do sometimes surface, and take flight.

Darkness lies just beyond or just inside. It's all in who and where you are...

THE CONQUEROR WORM

Edgar Allan Poe, 1838

LO! 'TIS A GALA NIGHT
Within the lonesome latter years!
An angel throng, bewinged, bedight
In veils, and drowned in tears,
Sit in a theatre, to see
A play of hopes and fears,
While the orchestra breathes fitfully
The music of the spheres.

Mimes, in the form of God on high,
Mutter and mumble low,
And hither and thither fly—
Mere puppets they, who come and go
At bidding of vast formless things
That shift the scenery to and fro,
Flapping from out their Condor wings
Invisible Wo!

That motley drama—oh, be sureIt shall not be forgot!
With its Phantom chased for evermore,

By a crowd that seize it not,
Through a circle that ever returneth in
To the self-same spot,
And much of Madness, and more of Sin,
And Horror the soul of the plot.

But see, amid the mimic rout
A crawling shape intrude!
A blood-red thing that writhes from out
The scenic solitude!
It writhes!—it writhes!—with mortal pangs
The mimes become its food,
And the angels sob at vermin fangs
In human gore imbued.

Out—out are the lights—out all!
And, over each quivering form,
The curtain, a funeral pall,
Comes down with the rush of a storm,
And the angels, all pallid and wan,
Uprising, unveiling, affirm
That the play is the tragedy, "Man,"
And its hero the Conqueror Worm.

When Coldness Wraps This Suffering Clay

George Gordon (Lord) Byron, 1815

When coldness wraps this suffering clay,
Ah ! whither strays the immortal mind ?
It cannot die, it cannot stay,
But leaves its darkened dust behind.
Then, unembodied, doth it trace
By steps each planet's heavenly way ?
Or fill at once the realms of space,
A thing of eyes, that all survey ?
Eternal —- boundless —- undecayed,
A thought unseen, but seeing all,
All, all in earth, or skies displayed,
Shall it survey, shall it recall:
Each fainter trace that Memory holds
So darkly of departed years,
In one broad glance the Soul beholds,
And all, that was, at once appears.
Before Creation peopled earth,
Its eye shall roll through chaos back;

And where the farthest heaven had birth,

The Spirit trace its rising track.

And where the future mars or makes,

Its glance dilate o'er all to be,

While sun is quenched —- or System breaks,

Fixed in its own Eternity.

Above or Love —- Hope —- Hate —- or Fear,

It lives all passionless and pure:

An age shall fleet like earthly year;

Its years as moments shall endure.

Away —- away —- without a wing.

O'er all —- through all —- its thought shall fly,

A nameless and eternal thing,

Forgetting what it was to die.

SONNET: A DIRGE OF VICTORY

Edward Plunkett (Lord Dunsany), 1919

LIFT NOT THY TRUMPET, VICTORY, TO THE sky,
Nor through battalions nor by batteries blow,
But over hollows full of old wire go,
Where among dregs of war the long-dead lie
With wasted iron that the guns passed by.
When they went eastwards like a tide at flow;
There blow thy trumpet that the dead may know,
Who waited for thy coming, Victory.

It is not we that have deserved thy wreath,
They waited there among the towering weeds.
The deep mud burned under the thermite's breath,
And winter cracked the bones that no man heeds:
Hundreds of nights flamed by: the seasons passed.
And thou last come to them at last, at last!

THE FEAR

Robert Frost, 1914

A LANTERN LIGHT FROM DEEPER IN THE
barn
Shone on a man and woman in the door
And threw their lurching shadows on a house
Nearby, all dark in every glossy window.
A horse's hoof pawed once the hollow floor,
And the back of the gig they stood beside
Moved in a little. The man grasped a wheel,
The woman spoke out sharply, "Whoa, stand still!"
"I saw it just as plain as a white plate,"
She said, "as the light on the dashboard ran
Along the bushes at the roadside—a man's face.
You must have seen it too."
"I didn't see it.
Are you sure——"
"Yes, I'm sure!"
"—it was a face?"
"Joel, I'll have to look. I can't go in,
I can't, and leave a thing like that unsettled.

Doors locked and curtains drawn will make no
    difference.
I always have felt strange when we came home
To the dark house after so long an absence,
And the key rattled loudly into place
Seemed to warn someone to be getting out
At one door as we entered at another.
What if I'm right, and someone all the time—
Don't hold my arm!"
"I say it's someone passing."
"You speak as if this were a travelled road.
You forget where we are. What is beyond
That he'd be going to or coming from
At such an hour of night, and on foot too.
What was he standing still for in the bushes?"
"It's not so very late—it's only dark.
There's more in it than you're inclined to say.
Did he look like——?"
"He looked like anyone.
I'll never rest to-night unless I know.
Give me the lantern."
"You don't want the lantern."
She pushed past him and got it for herself.
"You're not to come," she said. "This is my business.
If the time's come to face it, I'm the one
To put it the right way. He'd never dare—

Listen! He kicked a stone. Hear that, hear that!
He's coming towards us. Joel, go in—please.
Hark!—I don't hear him now. But please go in."
"In the first place you can't make me believe it's——"
"It is—or someone else he's sent to watch.
And now's the time to have it out with him
While we know definitely where he is.
Let him get off and he'll be everywhere
Around us, looking out of trees and bushes
Till I sha'n't dare to set a foot outdoors.
And I can't stand it. Joel, let me go!"
"But it's nonsense to think he'd care enough."
"You mean you couldn't understand his caring.
Oh, but you see he hadn't had enough—
Joel, I won't—I won't—I promise you.
We mustn't say hard things. You mustn't either."
"I'll be the one, if anybody goes!
But you give him the advantage with this light.
What couldn't he do to us standing here!
And if to see was what he wanted, why
He has seen all there was to see and gone."
He appeared to forget to keep his hold,
But advanced with her as she crossed the grass.
"What do you want?" she cried to all the dark.
She stretched up tall to overlook the light
That hung in both hands hot against her skirt.

"There's no one; so you're wrong," he said.

"There is.—

What do you want?" she cried, and then herself

Was startled when an answer really came.

"Nothing." It came from well along the road.

She reached a hand to Joel for support:

The smell of scorching woollen made her faint.

"What are you doing round this house at night?"

"Nothing." A pause: there seemed no more to say.

And then the voice again: "You seem afraid.

I saw by the way you whipped up the horse.

I'll just come forward in the lantern light

And let you see."

"Yes, do.—Joel, go back!"

She stood her ground against the noisy steps

That came on, but her body rocked a little.

"You see," the voice said.

"Oh." She looked and looked.

"You don't see—I've a child here by the hand."

"What's a child doing at this time of night——?"

"Out walking. Every child should have the memory

Of at least one long-after-bedtime walk.

What, son?"

"Then I should think you'd try to find

Somewhere to walk——"

"The highway as it happens—

We're stopping for the fortnight down at Dean's."
"But if that's all—Joel—you realize—
You won't think anything. You understand?
You understand that we have to be careful.
This is a very, very lonely place.
Joel!" She spoke as if she couldn't turn.
The swinging lantern lengthened to the ground,
It touched, it struck it, clattered and went out.

THE RAVEN

Samuel Taylor Coleridge, 1797

UNDER THE ARMS OF A GOODLY OAK-tree,

    There was of Swine a large company.

They were making a rude repast,

Grunting as they crunch'd the mast.

Then they trotted away: for the wind blew high—

One acorn they left, ne more mote you spy.

Next came a Raven, who lik'd not such folly;

He belong'd, I believe, to the witch Melancholy!

Blacker was he than the blackest jet;

Flew low in the rain; his feathers were wet.

He pick'd up the acorn and buried it strait,

By the side of a river both deep and great.

Where then did the Raven go?

He went high and low—

O'er hill, o'er dale did the black Raven go!

Many Autumns, many Springs;

Travell'd he with wand'ring wings;

Many Summers, many Winters—

I can't tell half his adventures.

At length he return'd, and with him a she;
And the acorn was grown a large oak-tree.
They built them a nest in the topmost bough,
And young ones they had, and were jolly enow.
But soon came a Woodman in leathern guise:
His brow like a pent-house hung over his eyes.
He'd an axe in his hand, and he nothing spoke,
But with many a hem! and a sturdy stroke,
At last he brought down the poor Raven's own oak.
His young ones were kill'd, for they could not depart,
And his wife she did die of a broken heart!
The branches from off it the Woodman did sever!
And they floated it down on the course of the River:
They saw'd it to planks, and it's rind they did strip,
And with this tree and others they built up a ship.
The ship, it was launch'd; but in sight of the land,
A tempest arose which no ship could withstand.
It bulg'd on a rock, and the waves rush'd in fast—
The auld Raven flew round and round, and caw'd to
    the blast.
He heard the sea-shriek of their perishing souls—
They be sunk! O'er the top-mast the mad water rolls.
The Raven was glad that such fate they did meet,
They had taken his all, and Revenge was Sweet!

ANGEL BY MICHAEL BIELACZYC

URIEL

Ralph Waldo Emerson, 1847

IT FELL IN THE ANCIENT PERIODS
Which the brooding soul surveys,
Or ever the wild Time coined itself
Into calendar months and days.
This was the lapse of Uriel,
Which in Paradise befell.
Once among the Pleiads walking,
Said overheard the young gods talking,
And the treason too long pent
To his ears was evident.
The young deities discussed
Laws of form and metre just,
Orb, quintessence, and sunbeams,
What subsisteth, and what seems.
One, with low tones that decide,
And doubt and reverend use defied,
With a look that solved the sphere,
And stirred the devils everywhere,
Gave his sentiment divine
Against the being of a line:

"Line in nature is not found,
Unit and universe are round;
In vain produced, all rays return,
Evil will bless, and ice will burn."
As Uriel spoke with piercing eye,
A shudder ran around the sky;
The stern old war-gods shook their heads,
The seraphs frowned from myrtle-beds;
Seemed to the holy festival,
The rash word boded ill to all;
The balance-beam of Fate was bent;
The bonds of good and ill were rent;
Strong Hades could not keep his own,
But all slid to confusion.
A sad self-knowledge withering fell
On the beauty of Uriel.
In heaven once eminent, the god
Withdrew that hour into his cloud,
Whether doomed to long gyration
In the sea of generation,
Or by knowledge grown too bright
To hit the nerve of feebler sight.
Straightway a forgetting wind
Stole over the Celestial kind,
And their lips the secret kept,
If in ashes the fibre-seed slept.

But now and then truth-speaking things
Shamed the angels' veiling wings,
And, shrilling from the solar course,
Or from fruit of chemic force,
Procession of a soul in matter,
Or the speeding change of water,
Or out of the good of evil born,
Came Uriel's voice of cherub scorn;
And a blush tinged the upper sky,
And the gods shook, they knew not why.

THE DIVISION SUPERINTENDENT

Ambrose Bierce, 1903

BAFFLED HE STANDS UPON THE TRACK—
The automatic switches clack.
Where'er he turns his solemn eyes
The interlocking signals rise.
The trains, before his visage pale,
Glide smoothly by, nor leave the rail.
No splinter-spitted victim he
Hears uttering the note high C.
In sorrow deep he hangs his head,
A-weary—would that he were dead.
Now suddenly his spirits rise—
A great thought kindles in his eyes.
Hope, like a headlight's vivid glare,
Splendors the path of his despair.
His genius shines, the clouds roll back—
"I'll place obstructions on the track!"

SILENCE
Richard Groller

SPEAK TO DARKNESS, SPEAK TO THE NIGHT,
if you listen in silence, you'll hear what's right.
You have your freedom, but not much time,
your apathy's a horrendous crime.
You dream you fools–believing, not knowing!
Praying and gazing, longing and hoping,
you will die for a sin of the very worst kind -
protecting one's heart from one's own mind.
By refusing all truth, whatever it may be
you will soon be damned for eternity.

Speak to darkness, speak to the night,
for in silence you'll ever lose your fight.
Go, drain the mind and cleanse the soul,
and once again be of spirit whole.
His satanic majesty's fight has begun,
and it seems as if he's already won.
For all his damned psychology
of free men has made a mockery;
and without a valiant Christian stand,

freedom shall slip right through your hand.

Speak to darkness, speak to the night,
in silence is all evil's might.
I do not know if it's love I feel,
for my eyes are blind and the world unreal.
I watch you suffer, I see you bleed,
in the past my words you would never heed.
And you now realize your big mistake,
and you pray to God for your soul to take,
and you've learned hard now through your tortured
    cries,
every sound must end in silence, but the silence never
    dies.

THE LAST PRAYER OF A DAMNED SOUL

Jack William Finley

HELL BECKONS AND I WAIT, COUNTING the days, a one way ticket clutched in my wretched hands

A soul blackened by hate and rage and despair, I have
only myself to blame

My sins come 'round again to haunt me in this
darkest hour, all the things I should have done

All the people I let down and betrayed.

I am the great deceiver the liar, the cheat, breaker of
innocent hearts and corrupter of souls

My heart is empty, barren cracked and broken like
dried out desert sand.

And the world is better for it, for my soul was a
wicked and evil instrument of torture

No one who ever knew it in its truest form was ever
better for it

I am the Pied Piper of Lost Souls, leading the damned
to a fate none deserve more than I

My sins have come home to me now, to lie on my
    chest like cold black boulders crushing the breathe
    from my wicked evil body, purging me once and
    for all of the breath of life I so wantonly abused
The end is nearly upon me and I welcome it, I grow
    tired of this masquerade pretending I deserve
    better, pretending I'm a better man than I am
Dear god in heaven strike me down and be done with
    it, I have burdened this world with enough sorrow

End me now and let me leave the world in peace to
    join the other monsters in the fate we have earned
Endless torment is too good for me but at least I know
    in death I can do no more harm.

SATYR'S ORISON

Richard Groller

THE MIDNIGHT HOUR IS CALLING NOW,
the full moon fills the sky.
My heart is warm though the night is chill,
I want you by my side.
My yearning for you mars my soul,
within my dreams I howl.
In my mind's eye is a nightmare world,
I stalk with cape and cowl.

For your eyes they shimmer like fireflies,
alone in the forest of night,
and your hair it glows like a faerie's dream
to soothe all my fears of the light.

Your brightness shatters the earthlight;
your aura bathes my soul.
By the dark of the moon, it calls to me,
and draws me from deep in my hole.
On gossamer wings we breathed the night,
and walked the ocean of storms.

In your mirrored eyes, on the mount of the moon
I have seen my hideous form.

Yet your eyes are as warm as hearth light,
the blaze in the prism of my soul.
And your touch is as soft as the morning dew,
the love that alone keeps me whole.

The Black Star Traveling Show

Kurt Newton

WHEN THE BLACK STAR TRAVELING
Show comes to town,
dead birds dot the trail behind like bread
crumbs,
and flowers wither in their beds and fill the air
with their rancid fragrance.

When the Black Star Traveling Show comes to town,
men who never raised their hand against their wives
leave purple blossoms upon their loved ones' faces
and the seeds of hatred planted in their hearts.

When the Black Star Traveling Show comes to town,
it brings a cold, bone-chilling wind from the pit of
    space
that turns the sunlit skies grey with clouds
that hang low like a crushing anvil.

When the Black Star Traveling Show comes to town,
the night becomes a long and restless place
where the silent screams of fading dreams

join the creeping call of chaos.

AN ANCIENT INSANE GOD BY MICHAEL BIELACZYC

AN ANCIENT INSANE GOD

Michael H. Hanson

WE ARE EACH A COMPOSITION,
a poem written across decades;
solo arrangements of moments
and cumulative harmonies.

Some of us are a rich opus,
honeyed lyrical manuscripts
lauding wondrous accomplishments
born of elegant craftsmanship.

But what of those discordant ones
whose mistakes and losses clang on,
and on, we disharmonious,
noisy operas of failure?

Perhaps there are a lonely few,
Dadaist rants vaguely content.
But most, like me, are horrid songs
composed by ancient insane gods.

THE ILLUSTRATIONS OF ROBERT INGRAM PRICE

Kurt Newton

JEFFREY THOMAS WAS EATING TUNA FROM
a tin
when the stories arrived by post,
a bit of illustration work sent by a publisher friend,
a gift, a handout seen by most.
But Jeffrey's dignity was hard to bruise,
he was once as good as the rest,
before women and liquor fed his life to the blues
and the deadlines came and went unmet.

Illustrating these stories was his second chance
(more like third or fourth, truth be told),
so he went to the attic to find his pens
and found they were too worn and too old.

Without money for replacements, he'd have to make
due,
so he sat down and read the manuscript twice:
stories both realistically horrific and true

by the author Robert Ingram Price.

Price's life was as short-lived and fantastic as his
    words,
he'd been a practitioner of the occult,
until he disappeared, never again seen or heard,
until the discovery of these stories in a vault.

So Jeffrey began, as sober as sin,
drunk on Price's inspiration,
sketching and stippling away with his pens,
surprised at the quality of the illustrations.

It was as if his pens had returned to new,
as sharp and as crisp as before.
For Jeffrey, the question wasn't how such things could
    be true,
but rather, in this case, how long could it be ignored?

Panel after panel came to life beneath his hand,
one horrific image after the next,
creatures of the night both of the sky and the land,
as if birthed from the stories' text.

Until, at last, the illustrations were complete,
Jeffrey's pens now as fresh as the day they were
    bought.

From out of the shadows there came the shuffling of
 feet,
and Jeffrey turned to see what his efforts had
 wrought.

A curious little man, a hundred years lost,
stood there with a dark glint in his eye.
"Thank you, my friend," he spoke, then he paused,
before slipping through the wall out of sight.

Jeffrey Thomas had indeed been given a second
 chance,
and his pens stayed forever brilliant and bright.
His illustrations are now featured on every magazine
 stand,
thanks to the helping hand of Robert Ingram Price.

THE GRAVE OF THE HUNDRED HEAD

Rudyard Kipling, 1888

THERE'S A WIDOW IN SLEEPY CHESTER
Who weeps for her only son;
There's a grave on the Pabeng River,
A grave that the Burmans shun,
And there's Subadar Prag Tewarri
Who tells how the work was done.
A Snider squibbed in the jungle,
Somebody laughed and fled,
And the men of the First Shikaris
Picked up their Subaltern dead,
With a big blue mark in his forehead
And the back blown out of his head.
Subadar Prag Tewarri,
Jemadar Hira Lal,
Took command of the party,
Twenty rifles in all,
Marched them down to the river
As the day was beginning to fall.

They buried the boy by the river,
A blanket over his face—
They wept for their dead Lieutenant,
The men of an alien race—
They made a samadh in his honor,
A mark for his resting-place.
For they swore by the Holy Water,
They swore by the salt they ate,
That the soul of Lieutenant Eshmitt Sahib
Should go to his God in state;
With fifty file of Burman
To open him Heaven's gate.
The men of the First Shikaris
Marched till the break of day,
Till they came to the rebel village,
The village of Pabengmay—
A jingal covered the clearing,
Calthrops hampered the way.
Subadar Prag Tewarri,
Bidding them load with ball,
Halted a dozen rifles
Under the village wall;
Sent out a flanking-party
With Jemadar Hira Lal.
The men of the First Shikaris
Shouted and smote and slew,

Turning the grinning jingal
On to the howling crew.
The Jemadar's flanking-party
Butchered the folk who flew.
Long was the morn of slaughter,
Long was the list of slain,
Five score heads were taken,
Five score heads and twain;
And the men of the First Shikaris
Went back to their grave again,
Each man bearing a basket
Red as his palms that day,
Red as the blazing village—
The village of Pabengmay,
And the "drip-drip-drip" from the baskets
Reddened the grass by the way.
They made a pile of their trophies
High as a tall man's chin,
Head upon head distorted,
Set in a sightless grin,
Anger and pain and terror
Stamped on the smoke-scorched skin.
Subadar Prag Tewarri
Put the head of the Boh
On the top of the mound of triumph,
The head of his son below,

With the sword and the peacock-banner
That the world might behold and know.
Thus the samadh was perfect,
Thus was the lesson plain
Of the wrath of the First Shikaris—
The price of a white man slain;
And the men of the First Shikaris
Went back into camp again.
Then a silence came to the river,
A hush fell over the shore,
And Bohs that were brave departed,
And Sniders squibbed no more;
For the Burmans said
That a kullah's head
Must be paid for with heads five score.
There's a widow in sleepy Chester
Who weeps for her only son;
There's a grave on the Pabeng River,
A grave that the Burmans shun,
And there's Subadar Prag Tewarri
Who tells how the work was done.

Sonnet: "Oh! Death Will Find Me, Long Before I Tire"

Rupert Brooke, 1911

OH! DEATH WILL FIND ME, LONG BEFORE
I tire
Of watching you; and swing me suddenly
Into the shade and loneliness and mire
Of the last land! There, waiting patiently,

One day, I think, I'll feel a cool wind blowing,
See a slow light across the Stygian tide,
And hear the Dead about me stir, unknowing,
And tremble. And I shall know that you have died,

And watch you, a broad-browed and smiling dream,
Pass, light as ever, through the lightless host,
Quietly ponder, start, and sway, and gleam —
Most individual and bewildering ghost! —

And turn, and toss your brown delightful head
Amusedly, among the ancient Dead.

SACRED NIGHT

Michelangelo Buonarroti, (1475-1564)

(rhymed English translation by John Addington Symonds, 1878)

ALL HOLLOW VAULTS AND DUNGEONS
sealed from sight,
All caverns circumscribed with roof and wall,
Defend dark Night, though noon around her fall,
From the fierce play of solar day-beams bright.
But if she be assailed by fire or light,
Her powers divine are nought; they tremble all
Before things far more vile and trivial—
Even a glow-worm can confound their might.
The earth that lies bare to the sun, and breeds
A thousand germs that burgeon and decay—
This earth is wounded by the ploughman's share:
But only darkness serves for human seeds;
Night therefore is more sacred far than day,
Since man excels all fruits however fair.

INSANITY

Jillian A. Perkins

WORDS FLOWING FROM A SOUL THAT'S
been recently unlocked
Like blood pouring freely from a gash in a
rock
The manipulation that came from your selfish greed
Has rooted inside you the devils own seed

The pain you choke on when you try to feel pleasure
Comes from the hate for your love's futile endeavor
You think the world knows nothing of pain
So you have thoughts of vengeance etched into your
brain

Society must pay for the void in your heart
You've employed yourself to the Prince of the Dark
You walk the night stealing men's souls
With a hunger for blood, forever you'll roam

You're the cause of your own pain and despair
Yet you still look for sympathy, those who will care

You feel too little and think too much
Your heart isn't open; your soul can't be touched

You're always insensitive to the things you should
    love
And you justify all the acts of cruelty you've done
You're surrounded by people but you're still all alone
Your head is the only thing you truly call home

Inside your thoughts are the feelings of dread
Things that inspire fear all trapped in your head
Your heart is tainted, your emotions all gone
You're like a machine that's been left on too long

Did you do something wrong, or is it all in your mind
Are you beating yourself up for uncommitted crimes?
A made up reality is all that you know
Your feelings of guilt still continue to grow

Death is the friend that you long to find
To take you with him, away from your mind
You struggle to survive, your actions are to undo
Or kill the nightmare, the nightmare of you

TEARS

Bill Snider

THE DARKNESS SHEDS A TEAR
A word, a worry I never hear
Children whisper, quietly in fear
And not a thought is left that isn't dear.

Tumult and discord rampant
Throughout the realm of Earth
Of the large of the land to the small
Tangents of emotion clear and discard.

The darkness stands taken aback
Fearful of the light that threatens attack
Piss and vinegar, unholy violence on track
Fire and brimstone appearing through cracks.

Children of the streets mobbing the temples
Seeking simple salvation from starvation and woe
No corner of the land safe from these depredations
As the enemy comes nearer with a heavy, looming
tread.

The darkness is fighting for its life
Against the very thing that births strife
An abomination of contrivance and un-life
Things that wields a stick, a stone and a knife.

Nighttime Forest

Kimberly Richardson

A DARKENED FOREST DURING THE DAY
Is surreal – swirled into infinite
Dreams and tales of what once
Was. Silence under a dull
Knife is probably one's better option
Hidden deep within folds
Of fat and muscle, dirt and
Tissue. A rich fat layer
Dyed black and blue is
At home here in the forest
Of nightmares and screams
From women who gave up too soon.
My blood is thick and coarse
But it was never my intention
To see the forest fade.

Caves of Shame

Michael H. Hanson

I SEE LIFE WITH MONOCHROMATIC EYES,
surrounded by daguerreotype people;
silver shimmers in ghostly pale backgrounds,
distant wisps, ivory shadow puppets.

Condemned by overexposed rejection
I enter deep, long, underground caverns,
far from nature's judgmental cameras —
emotionally incorporeal.

I walk through subterranean valleys,
eyes downcast and sensitive to the light;
navigating by sorrowful laments,
shuttered in the dark chambers of my soul.

Breathless and fearful, I am a marching
empty exile reeking of damnation;
cast from above for common cowardice
to stagger within twilight confusion.

I am only mortal. I'm just a man.
I cannot break these Promethean chains...

FALLEN

Kimberly Richardson

REVELING IN THE BLOOD OF MY OWN
fallen body, my own enemy
To feel it in drops all over my body
And know that it does make a sound.

A glass of water: not enough

To convey my deepest apologies

That I have sinned, Father, bless my tongue with His
host

So that I may live once more

To drink from my glass of dead water.

Purity, denied.

OMNIA VINCIT AMOR

Dean M. Drinkel

OVEMENT INSIDE THE WOUND. THIS IS real.

The beetles, the roaches, the maggots.
A feast from the Gods, raise a glass to Bacchus.
Happy fervour for any morsel to satisfy the
Starving nation.

Amongst the carnage, a child cries. Rabid, the
    madness
Gestates. It lies lonely in the viscera.
One elongated arm now extended, its hand a claw.
Like a bird, scratching at its own flesh, searching
For an answer. Someone put it out of its misery.
In the trees, the rustle of the wind hides its scream.
This bark is ancient, flaking away as the
Breeze battles against it. A focal point for devilment,
For religious ecstasy as the sun breaks through
The canopy, casting shadows of light.

Hypocrisy also, for from its strongest branch
The naked woman hangs. Dead. What happened?

No-one is saying, all voices are silent, voices lost
Upon the air. A single flame heads Earthwards,
It too is famished, from flesh it has been starved.
The child waits, its mouth wide open, ready to ingest.

LINES ON SEEING SCHILLER'S SKULL

Johann Wolfgang von Goethe, 1820

Translation by Edgar A. Bowring, 1853

WITHIN A GLOOMY CHARNEL-HOUSE one day
    I view'd the countless skulls, so strangely mated,
And of old times I thought, that now were grey.
Close pack'd they stand, that once so fiercely hated,
And hardy bones, that to the death contended,
Are lying cross'd,—to lie for ever, fated.
What held those crooked shoulder-blades suspended?
No one now asks; and limbs with vigour fired,
The hand, the foot—their use in life is ended.
Vainly ye sought the tomb for rest when tired;
Peace in the grave may not be yours; ye're driven
Back into daylight by a force inspired;
But none can love the wither'd husk, though even
A glorious noble kernel it contained.
To me, an adept, was the writing given
Which not to all its holy sense explained,

When 'mid the crowd, their icy shadows flinging,

I saw a form, that glorious still remained.

And even there, where mould and damp were
    clinging,

Gave me a blest, a rapture-fraught emotion,

As though from death a living fount were springing.

What mystic joy I felt! What rapt devotion!

That form, how pregnant with a godlike trace!

A look, how did it whirl me tow'rd that ocean

Whose rolling billows mightier shapes embrace!

Mysterious vessel! Oracle how dear!

Even to grasp thee is my hand too base,

Except to steal thee from thy prison here

With pious purpose, and devoutly go

Back to the air, free thoughts, and sunlight clear.

What greater gain in life can man e'er know

Than when God-Nature will to him explain

How into Spirit steadfastness may flow,

How steadfast, too, the Spirit-Born remain.

In the City of Beggars

Dean M. Drinkel

DAWNING LIKE EYES OPENING.
The click and the whirl of the copper insect
At your ear – it promises starlight.
But the darkness as a blanket wraps
Itself around you suggests a hyper- reality.

In the belly of the whale, you smile through
 graveyard teeth.
Did we still believe this was true? The bruises, broken
 bones,
Bloodied wounds said yes, this was real life, enjoy it.
It is our strength that keeps at bay the bowels of the
 Earth,
There we go, tip toeing through the fields of broken
 glass.

Still we pledge our allegiance. But God doesn't
 understand us.
Ignores the pain and suffering we endure in His name.
As I snap your fingers, cleave your flesh,

Feast on your brain, I offer thanks that I have been
chosen

To fight on His side – imagine the alternative.

When I am done, I float towards the mouth of the
beast,

One brief moment to turn and see already you have
been

Swallowed by the sun. Did you ever exist in the first
place,

Or were you just a figment of my imagination? I feel
the

Child grow within and as my tears turn to ice, I
realise it

Is my turn to face the music and vomited onto the
Earth I am.

INVICTUS

William Ernest Henley, 1875

OUT OF THE NIGHT THAT COVERS ME,
Black as the Pit from pole to pole,
I thank whatever gods may be
For my unconquerable soul.

In the fell clutch of circumstance
I have not winced nor cried aloud.
Under the bludgeonings of chance
My head is bloody, but unbowed.

Beyond this place of wrath and tears
Looms but the Horror of the shade,
And yet the menace of the years
Finds, and shall find, me unafraid.

It matters not how strait the gate,
How charged with punishments the scroll,
I am the master of my fate:
I am the captain of my soul.

HOVERING SCAVENGER BY LIZ HOLLAND

ARTIST ATTRIBUTIONS
IN ORDER OF APPEARANCE:

THE GARDEN OF GOOD AND GOOD, ©Chris Mars,
Chris Mars Publishing

BOOK OF NIGHT FRONTISPIECE, ©2014 Bob Giadrosich,
Brush/Ink

APPARITIONS, ©2011 Bob Giadrosich, Brush/Ink

FOLLOW ME, ©2011 Paul Bielaczyc, Ink

THE SHADOW PEOPLE, ©2011 Bob Giadrosich,
Brush/Ink

AUTUMN PEOPLE, ©2011 Bob Giadrosich, Brush/Ink

MOON ON TREE TOP, ©2011 Liz Holland, Digital

FAERIE FIRE, ©2011 Michael Bielaczyc, Ink

MURDER'S CALL, ©2011 Paul Bielaczyc, Ink

LILITH, ©2011 Michael Bielaczyc, 2011, Ink

SWEET SORROW, ©2011 Bob Giadrosich, Brush/Ink

TIL DEATH, ©2011 Paul Bielaczyc, Graphite

PUMPKIN IN THE SKY, ©2011 Liz Holland, Digital

DYING INSIDE, © 2011 Bob Giadrosich, Brush/Ink

ANGEL, © 2011 Michael Bielaczyc, Ink

AN ANCIENT INSANE GOD, © 2011 Michael Bielaczyc,

HOVERING SCAVENGER, © 2011 Liz Holland, Digital

ARTIST CONTACT INFORMATION:

Contact the artists featured in "The Book of Night" at their websites, listed below.

Bob Giadrosich—
website: www.xiangbalastudio.com

Paul Bielaczyc—
website: www.aradani.com
email: paul@aradani.com

Michael Bielaczyc—
website: michaelbielaczyc.com

Liz Holland:
website: Facebook.com/pages/Digital-Doodles/

Chris Mars/Chris Mars Publishing Inc.
www.chrismarspublishing.com

Citations
Apparitions

Edgar Allan Poe (1809-1849), "Dream-Land", *Graham's Magazine*, George R. Graham, Philadelphia, June 1844

George Gordon (Lord) Byron (1788-1824), "Darkness", *The Prisoner of Chillon and Other Poems*, John Murray, London, 1816

Robert Frost (1874-1963), "The Demiurge's Laugh", *A Boy's Will*, Henry Holt and Co., 1915

Samuel Taylor Coleridge (1772-1834) "Love's Apparition and Evanishment", *The Complete Poetical Works of Samuel Taylor Coleridge, Vol. 1: Poems,* Edited by Ernest Hartley Coleridge, Oxford at the Clarendon Press, Henry Frowde, Publisher to the University of Oxford, London, Edinburgh, New York, 1912

Ambrose Bierce (1842-1913), "A Vision of Doom", *Shapes of Clay*, W.E. Wood: San Francisco, 1903

Ralph Waldo Emerson (1803-1882), "Peter's Field", *Poems* , The Riverside Press, Cambridge, Houghton Mifflin and Company, Boston, 1886

Ambrose Bierce (1842-1913), From "The Death of Halpin Frayser", *Can Such Things Be?*, The Cassell Publishing Co., New York, 1893

Rudyard Kipling (1865-1936), "En-Dor", *The Years Between,* Methuen and Co. LTD, London, 1919

Rupert Brooke (1887-1915), "The Call", *The Collected Poems of Rupert Brook*, John Lane, New York and London, 1915

Edgar Allan Poe (1809-1849), "The Bells", *Sartrain's Union Magazine*, John Sartain, Philadelphia, November 1849

Johann Wolfgang von Goethe, (1749-1832), " Dance of the Dead", Translation by Edgar A. Bowring, (1826-1911), *The Poems of Goethe*, Hurst & Company Publishers, New York, 1853

AUTUMN PEOPLE

Edgar Allan Poe (1809-1849), "Ulalume", *American Whig Review*, George H. Colton, New York, 1847

Robert Frost (1874-1963), "My November Guest", *A Boy's Will*, Henry Holt and Co., 1915

Samuel Taylor Coleridge (1772-1834) "Sonnet: To The Autumnal Moon", *The Complete Poetical Works of Samuel Taylor Coleridge, Vol. 1: Poems,* Edited by Ernest Hartley Coleridge, Oxford at the Clarendon Press, Henry Frowde, Publisher to the University of Oxford, London, Edinburgh, New York, 1912

Ambrose Bierce (1842-1913), "Constancy", *Shapes of Clay*, W.E. Wood, San Francisco, 1903

Rupert Brooke (1887-1915), " The Life Beyond ", *Poems*, Sidgwick & Jackson Limited, London, 1911

SWEET SORROW

Edgar Allan Poe (1809-1849), "Annabel Lee", *New York Daily Tribune*, Greeley and McElrath, New York, October 9, 1849

George Gordon (Lord) Byron (1788-1824), "And Thou Art Dead, As Young and Fair", *Childe Harold's Pilgrimage. A Romaunt,* Second Edition, John Murray, London, 1812

George Gordon (Lord) Byron (1788-1824), "Love and Death", *Murray's Magazine,* John Murray, London, February 1887

Robert Frost (1874-1963), ""Out, Out -"", *Mountain Interval*, Henry Holt and Co., 1916

Samuel Taylor Coleridge (1772-1834) "The Pang More Sharp Than All. An Allegory", *The Complete Poetical Works of Samuel Taylor Coleridge, Vol. 1: Poems,* Edited by Ernest Hartley Coleridge, Oxford at the Clarendon Press, Henry Frowde, Publisher to the University of Oxford, London, Edinburgh, New York, 1912

Ambrose Bierce (1842-1913), "Vice Versa", *Shapes of Clay*, W.E. Wood: San Francisco, 1903

Johann Wolfgang von Goethe, (1749-1832), "To the Rising Full Moon", Translation by Edgar A.

Bowring, (1826-1911), *The Poems of Goethe*, Hurst & Company Publishers, New York, 1853

Rudyard Kipling (1865-1936), "The Moon of Other Days" *Departmental Ditties, Barrack-Room Ballads, and Other Verses,* John W. Lovell Company, New York, 1890

Rupert Brooke (1887-1915), "The Visions of the Archangels", *The Collected Poems of Rupert Brook,* John Lane, New York and London, 1915

Oscar Wilde (1854-1900) "Requiescat", *Poems*, Robert Brothers, Boston, 1881

Johann Wolfgang von Goethe, (1749-1832), "The Erl-King", Translation by Edgar A. Bowring, (1826-1911), *The Poems of Goethe*, Hurst & Company Publishers, New York, 1853

THROUGH A GLASS DARKLY

Edgar Allan Poe (1809-1849), "The Conqueror Worm", *Graham's Magazine*, George R. Graham, Philadelphia, January1843

George Gordon (Lord) Byron (1788-1824), "When Coldness Wraps This Suffering Clay", *Hebrew Melodies,* John Murray, London, 1815

Edward J.M.D. Plunkett, (Lord Dunsany) (1878-1957), "A Dirge of Victory", *Unhappy Far-Off Things,* Elkin Matthews, London, 1919

Robert Frost (1874-1963), "The Fear", *North of Boston*, David Nutt Publishing, 1914

Samuel Taylor Coleridge (1772-1834) "The Raven", *The Complete Poetical Works of Samuel Taylor Coleridge, Vol. 1: Poems,* Edited by Ernest Hartley Coleridge, Oxford at the Clarendon Press, Henry Frowde, Publisher to the University of Oxford, London, Edinburgh, New York, 1912

Ambrose Bierce (1842-1913), " The Division Superintendent", *Shapes of Clay*, W.E. Wood: San Francisco, 1903

Ralph Waldo Emerson (1803-1882), "Uriel", *Poems*, The Riverside Press, Cambridge, Houghton Mifflin and Company, Boston, 1886

Rudyard Kipling (1865-1936), " The Grave of the Hundred Head " *Departmental Ditties, Barrack-Room Ballads, and Other Verses,* John W. Lovell Company, New York, 1890

Rupert Brooke (1887-1915), "Oh! Death Will Find Me, Long Before I Tire", *Poems,* Sidgwick & Jackson Limited, London, 1911

Michelangelo Buonarroti (1475-1564), "Sacred Night" *The Sonnets of Michael Angelo Buonarroti and Tommaso Campanella,* (rhymed English translation by John Addington Symonds, (1840-1893), Smith, Elder & Co., London, 1878

Johann Wolfgang von Goethe, (1749-1832), "Lines on Seeing Schiller's Skull", Translation by Edgar A. Bowring, (1826-1911), *The Poems of Goethe,* Hurst & Company Publishers, New York, 1853

William Ernest Henley (1849-1903), "Invictus", *The Oxford Book of English Verse 1250-1900,* edited by A.T. Quiller-Couch, Oxford at the Clarendon Press, Henry Frowde, Publisher to the University of Oxford, London, Edinburgh, New York, 1902

Copper Dog Publishing LLC

OUR IMPRINTS

MoonDream
PRESS

SCIENCE FICTION, HORROR AND FANTASY

RACKET RIVER Press

POETRY

Pumpkin Hill Press

CHILDRENS' TITLES

To find out more about our imprints
and our upcoming releases, visit our website:
www.CopperDogPublishing.com
or our Facebook page:
www.facebook.com/copperdogpublishing

www.ingramcontent.com/pod-product-compliance
Lightning Source LLC
Chambersburg PA
CBHW050458260626
47157CB00004B/1107